I0460678

THE LADY OF SHALOTT

A Novel

THE LADY OF SHALOTT

A Novel

Stephanie McGann

©2019 Stephanie McGann
All rights reserved

Arc Publishing, LLC
College Park, MD

First Edition
ISBN 978-1-7329602-1-3
Library of Congress Control Number:
2019900369

This is a work of fiction. Names, characters, places, and incidents either are the products of the author's imagination or are used fictitiously. Any resemblance to actual persons, living or dead, businesses, companies, events, or locales is entirely coincidental.

Cover design by Adina McGee

AUTHOR'S NOTE

The following story takes its inspiration from the legend of King Arthur and Sir Alfred Lord Tennyson's poem, "The Lady of Shalott." I have borrowed sections of Tennyson's poem to use for some of the spells. For others, I have attempted to match his style, meter, and rhyme scheme. The songs I have included are derived from the Middle Ages. In order of appearance, they are stanza seven of the "The Unquiet Grave" whose author is unknown, stanza one and the chorus of "Greensleves," often attributed to King Henry VIII, and stanza four of "O Sacred Head Now Wounded" by Saint Bernard of Clairvaux and others. The opening lines of each part of the book come from Dante Alighieri's *Divine Comedy*.

To My Husband

PART I

The Nunnery

When I had journeyed half of our life's way,
I found myself within a shadowed forest,
for I had lost the path that does not stray.
Ah, it is hard to speak of what it was,
that savage forest, dense and difficult,
which even in recall renews my fear:
so bitter—death is hardly more severe!

- DANTE ALIGHIERI, *THE DIVINE COMEDY*,
CANTO I, VERSES 1-7

1

It was a black day, but not so black as the many days before. Morgana had finally resigned to accept her place in the nunnery, to live in the shadows of its cloistered walls. With this came a type of empowerment, a sense she could still control her fate even if others thought she was but a thirteen-year-old girl to be chided.

No, she would never have chosen to enter the convent of her own will, even under the pretext that it was merely for schooling. She had fought her mother at first, but soon realized there was no point in arguing since the decision had been made by her step-father, Uther Pendragron, King of Britain. How she despised him! Her mother may be fooled, but Morgana surely was not. Uther, as she insisted on calling him behind his back, was nothing more than a churl, a hedge-born cockscomb, a crooked-nosed knave, a liver-eatin craven…It felt good to fling a few insults, even if they just echoed through her mind.

"Dong! Dong!" rang out the bells announcing prime.

Its heavy toll jolted Morgana into motion. She splashed cold water on her face and reluctantly set off to join morning prayer.

To her surprise, a new novice was kneeling before the altar. Distracted, Morgana's lips moved along to the prayers by rote, but her attention was fixed on the young lady. She was dressed in the same attire as herself, wearing a dull, greyish-black habit with a white scapular and simple veil adorning her face. In the dim sea of habits, the newcomer nonetheless stood out. She was bent forward, nearly falling over the kneeler. Uncomfortable though she appeared, she managed to remain as still as the statues of the Virgin Mary and Saint Joseph that flanked the altar.

Only after the concluding verse, as the novices dispersed to begin their lessons, did the newcomer break her stillness. Turning, she revealed a belly round with child bulging over a delicate frame. She could not be more than a few weeks, perhaps a month at most, from giving birth. Her face was luminous, which made the purplish swollenness of her under-eyes stand out all the more. She looked only a year, maybe two, older than Morgana. The young women locked eyes for a moment, but Morgana quickly looked away, embarrassed she had been caught staring.

Days at the nunnery were generally spent in solemn prayer, quiet study, and arduous chores, so supper was relished by all as a chance to converse freely. No sooner did Morgana take her seat that evening, then she realized something was amiss.

The normal rhythm of voices was awkwardly stifled. As she perked up her ears, she caught snipits of gossip murmured in hushed voices.

"She was brought hither under the cover of night for shame on the family," whispered one.

"Her mother was weeping all the while, but her father was devoid of emotion," scoffed another under her breath.

"He even refused to bid her farewell," announced a voice with feigned sympathy.

"Poor child," oozed yet another mockingly, "not even fit to keep the baby."

Morgana's sense of injustice was set off. Had not this woman suffered enough? Must she now suffer the injurious eyes and mean-spirited calumny of these so-called "holy" ladies?

Pushing out her chair angrily, Morgana snapped, "Prithee, excuse me, Mother Superior. I am unworthy of sitting amongst such virtuous ladies. I must make confession."

Brimming with righteous indignation, Morgana curtsied and departed. Her head rang with the sound of her father's voice, telling her to stand up for the weak, the oppressed, to fight against those who would crush another. He would have never stood by and watched one so tortured, even if by words alone.

With every passing day, Morgana became all the more determined to get to know the new novice whose name she learned was Roselyn. Her interest was not for the sake of gossip or the wolfish drama the nunnery had come to devour at every meal, but in the hopes of finding a kindred spirit. Morgana imagined Roselyn full of rebellion and fire like herself. How else could she have landed in her predicament as an unwed mother? Perhaps they could be outcasts together. Her chance finally came when they were both assigned to weed the garden.

"How are you finding the nunnery?" inquired Morgana in a hushed voice, as she plunged her spade into the earth, attempting to dislodge a stubborn weed. She secretly pretended it was Uther. *That's for killing my father!*

"Mother Superior has been very kind to me," replied Roselyn distantly. Heavy with child, she must have been in pain as she worked over the hard earth.

"You are much more graceful than I was. When I first abideth hither, I stayed in my room for three days." The spade hacked away but with little or no effect on the root. *That's for stealing my mother!*

"What convinced you to finally come out?" inquired Roselyn, as her delicate fingers freed a patch of lilies from a weedy strangulation.

"My stomach," Morgana quipped as she landed the death blow. *That's for ruining my life!* She glared triumphantly at the mangled weed then realized she had missed much of the root.

Roselyn could not help but laugh at Morgana's remark, so funny as it seemed that hunger could get the better of the stubborn girl before her.

Seizing the opportunity, Morgana began to

open up. She explained how her mother had remarried after her father's death and how her stepfather had insisted on sending her away when a new child, a boy, was born on the Christmas last. Morgana packed her bags alone and traveled without an escort on no less an occasion than the Feast of the Epiphany. While others were making merry in honor of the Magi's gifts to the Christ Child, she was bumping along in a carriage and stewing with bitterness over the "gifts" she had been given.

"How did your blood father die?" Roselyn asked with a saddened look on her face. Memories of the heart-wrenching parting with her own father were fresh in her mind. Holding her belly, she thought, too, of her child's father.

"He was killed most cruelly," Morgana replied, neglecting to say by whom. Then, as she annihilated another weed, she added flatly, "I intend to avenge his death."

That's for everything else.

With a look of sympathy, Roselyn gave a slight nod. Was she nodding in approval, or simply acknowledging what had been said? Morgana was unsure, but the pronouncement did the trick. Having heard Morgana's story, Roselyn divulged her own tragic tale, one of a secret, ill-begotten love.

"We were to be married this Spring after my six-teenth birthday," Roselyn said in conclusion. "If only I had been stronger…"

"You are only human," Morgana responded, hoping to cheer her up. Infidelity was not that big of a deal in the royal court—so long as it stayed away from the open light.

"No, you are wrong to say that, though I know you mean well by it," Roselyn rebuffed unexpectedly. "Our Lord became human, showing that humans are not only capable of goodness but called to goodness. My actions were shameful and unworthy of mankind."

Morgana flushed. She wanted a friend so badly and had probably spoiled her chances. If only she could keep the conversation going.

"Is it true that the nuns will take your baby?" she fumbled.

"They intend to, but…" Roselyn's voice trailed off momentarily, and her eyes looked up to Heaven. "But, I have a feeling something else is in store for my baby."

Morgana tried to think of something more to say, anything, but she drew a blank. It was just as well. Roselyn was probably too virtuous, even as an unwed mother, to desire a friend like Morgana, anyway. Side by side, they continued weeding in silent contemplation: Roselyn lamenting the impending separation from her baby, Morgana destroying every weed in her path. Only this time, the weeds had become nuns, and Morgana was clearing an escape route for Roselyn to the one place she could think of that offered *real* sanctuary— Grandmother's house.

When the bells tolled calling the novices to prayer, Roselyn shifted her weight and pushed herself upright. Rubbing her sore back, she said simply, "It was nice chatting with you, Morgana. Perchance we could go to the market together come Sunday."

"I would like that very much." Morgana smiled. She loosened the grip on her spade, and the color flowed back to her knuckles.

2

Morgana and Roselyn trudged back from the market, the former weighed down by a large basket full of chards, spinach, and leeks for the week's porry, and the latter weighed down by her massive, swollen belly. The more they walked, the heavier Roselyn's breathing became, and the more frequently she needed to stop and rest. Morgana gave Roselyn her arm, and then her shoulder, before finally abandoning her basket altogether and offering her whole self. She could feel Roselyn's body go tense with pain and then limp with exhaustion every few steps. The baby was coming, and they were still over a mile from the convent. None of the other novices would even think to look for them since they had left the market well ahead of schedule.

Morgana's eyes scanned the area in desperation and rested upon a little cottage with a thatched roof about a hundred yards off. A black bird hopped along the sparse pathway, poking about for food. A greedy cow chewed and spat the grass. A cat dark as ink flipped its tail like a whip and guarded the front step. It was the only option Morgana could fathom, but her stomach turned at the thought of seeking refuge there. Had Roselyn heard the rumors, too? Either way, she submitted to Morgana's guidance and painfully shuffled onward toward the cottage, unaware of just how cruel a hand Fate had dealt them.

"Just a few steps more," Morgana urged as they started along the path. The bird danced in front of them for a moment and then flew on top of the cottage with mocking ease.

"I can't," Roselyn moaned. She held her stomach and crumpled into a ball on the ground.

Morgana tried to swallow, but her mouth was dry. "I am going to get help inside. I will only be gone for a moment."

Roselyn nodded, her gaze far-off, fixed on Heaven, and tried her best to recite the birthing words every expectant mother pressed into their minds.

Child, come forth a shining person, who dwells with God...

The cat glared at Morgana as she crossed the threshold of the dim cottage, and the door seemed to open on its own. She hesitated. Her heart pounded out a warning, but there was no turning back, no matter how scared she was. The fearsome lion Morgana pretended to be had long since run away and left a fearful child behind.

"Linens are on the table. Hot water is on the stove," croaked an old woman rocking steadily in the corner. "And best not forget the rose water, right over thither, little comfort though it ever brings."

Morgana felt the hair on the back of her neck tingle. She wanted to slink away, but Roselyn needed her. Father would have told her to be brave. He would have held her hand.

Morgana gathered the materials with her eyes downcast, vainly pleading for help from anyone but the spinster. She turned and faced the creaky gliders of the rocking chair. "I do not know what to do."

"I will guide you—when it is time. We best not rush the inevitable," was the cool, foreboding response. The old spinster took a long, cleansing breath, pulled herself upright, and glided to Roselyn with an air that defied her age.

Morgana delivered the baby as if in a trance. Was it minutes or hours? She would never know. Her memory was a blurry collection of fragments. Roselyn pushed. A baby cried. Then, Morgana had the vague notion something otherworldly occurred. Had she been a woman of faith, she would have seen the angels escorting her only friend to Heaven. As it was, she simply saw death. She could not even look at the beautiful baby girl Roselyn swaddled in her lifeless, ivory arms.

"My carriage is ready and waiting. Do what needs to be done," said the old spinster, forcing Morgana back to reality. "The driver is waiting."

Before she knew what was happening, Morgana held the baby and began walking toward the carriage where she saw a thin, specter-like man holding the reins. She was too numb to cry and too desperate to think clearly. Nothing made sense.

"Where…?"

"Where else but your grandmother's?" the

spinster replied with a sly look on her face.

Morgana stopped in her tracks as she recalled her fanciful scheme of whisking Roselyn away there. Her spine splintered with trepidation.

"The baby's name is Lilian," continued the old spinster. "She will flower like her mother. May her bloom last longer. Now, go. You must hurry!"

Morgana's mind raced faster than the changing terrain. How could Roselyn, a young lady so full of life only hours ago, now be dead? And what kind of God would take a life in the very act of giving it to another? Bowing her head in anguish, she looked down at the helpless baby in her arms—at...at... Lilian—and wondered if she had acted rightly in obeying the spinster. Should she turn back and go to the nunnery? Something urged her on.

Grandmother would know what to do. She would make everything better.

Having lost a child of her own, Morgana felt certain Grandmother would take pity on them and welcome them into her home. But how could the spinster have known her fanciful machinations? She had never spoken a word of it—not even to Roselyn.

The sound of Lilian crying forced Morgana to quiet her mind and focus on comforting the small babe instead. She frantically rummaged through the carriage and found a neatly packed basket, complete with a bottle and a jug of cow's milk. Lilian rooted around inconsolably for what seemed a tortuously long time before she eventually latched on. Pacified, the unlikely pair rocked back and forth over the bumpy terrain until they both nodded off to sleep.

Morgana awoke in the cool night as the carriage turned down a little road she recognized from her childhood. The familiar smell of honeysuckles filled her nostrils as she looked around by the light of the moon. Despite the cover of night, she could picture the area clearly in her head. Well she remembered the feel of the soft grass between her toes and the gentle babble of the water that ran through the pasture. And how could she forget the large oak tree she climbed over and over again with her father? The memory stung Morgana like a swarm of bees. Had it really been nearly five years since his death?

Morgana heaved a sigh and shifted her weight uncomfortably. Much as she wanted to see Grandmother, she was nervous about her midnight visit, a visit she had put off for as many years as her father had been dead. Perhaps she had been foolish in her plight to seek refuge there. It was too late to change course, though, for the carriage had all but arrived at the front door.

Bracing herself, Morgana whispered to Lilian, "I dreamed of your mother bringing you hither, but it was not to be. I shall stand in her place and look out for you; come what may."

"Whoa!" called the phantom driver, and the wheels rolled to a stop.

3

"Who is there? Show yourself!" demanded a voice the moment the door creaked open.

"Grandmother, it is I." Morgana crossed the threshold and walked into the dimly lit cottage, feigning courage with each step. "I have come to beg your assistance on a dire matter."

Grandmother coiled her Rosary into her pocket and added a log to the fire. The red embers licked it up in an instant and illuminated the room. The soft glow revealed a spacious cottage unchanged since Morgana last saw it. A massive wooden table sat squarely in the middle of the room. At times, it served as a counter; at others, it was for eating meals. Well Morgana remembered chopping meat and vegetables atop its grooved surface in preparation for one of Grandmother's delicious meals. Various mismatched wooden chairs were casually placed about the entire room, giving the otherwise immaculate space a comfortable, lived-in feeling. Cupboards lined the wall to her left with pots and pans hung neatly above. A large tapestry hung over the fireplace.

Morgana could still picture Grandmother, with her long silver braid falling down her shoulder, working on the massive loom in the corner and making the Garden of Eden come to life on its frame. The Tree of Knowledge surrounded by a chorus of flowers appeared as her nimble fingers danced across the warp strings to the sound of her own sad singing. Morgana's heart shivered as she recalled the words of Grandmother's favorite ballad.

The stalk is withered dry, my love,
so will our hearts decay;
So make yourself content, my love,
till God calls you away…

The words rang hollow as they fluttered through Morgana's mind and up the stairwell to the bed-rooms. How Morgana longed to rest her head on one of those soft feather beds! One look at Grand-mother's face, though, and Morgana knew rest would not come in the form of sleep anytime soon.

Grandmother's steely blue eyes narrowed at the sight of the newborn and then shifted intently to Morgana. There was no sign of puffiness in her face or form to suggest she had just given birth. Nor did she have even the slightest bearing of motherliness about her. Though Lilian was tucked tightly in her arms, Morgana looked stiff and awkward and scared.

"Morgana, whose child have you brought to my home in the middle of the night looking a daggle tail? Explain yourself," Grandmother said in a voice only a touch gentler than before.

"Grandmother, this child is named Lilian. She is

the newborn daughter of my dear friend Roselyn, who died this very day in childbirth. Having been sent to the nunnery against her will as punishment for the sin of adultery, the nuns laid claim to her baby. I could not let that happen, so I have come hither begging your help. I prithee, let us build a home for Lilian here," Morgana asked in earnest.

Grandmother's heart ached at the thought of a second chance to raise a child and to bring Morgana back into her life, but she was not ready to give in so easily. She had to press more firmly to ensure she would be right in doing so. Age had taught her things were not always as they seemed.

"Did this child's mother ask you to take her baby?" Grandmother questioned dubiously.

"No, but…" Morgana replied as she choked back tears. The emotions of the day and fatigue of the long journey were beginning to set in more fully. "I believe she would have wanted me to. She would have wanted her child to have a happy life."

"What makes you think the nuns had something different in mind? They are the Lord's servants. Surely, they would provide well for this child," Grandmother countered abruptly.

"Their version of happiness is not the same for everyone," Morgana replied indignantly, no longer thinking about Lilian's future but her own. Her eyes glared more deeply than the smoldering embers in the fireplace as she went on, "The convent is a paradise for some but a hell for others. Why not let this child choose her own path? Why punish her for…"

The mistakes of another.

Morgana could not get the words out. She had cared so much for Roselyn in the short time they had known one another; Morgana did not believe her capable of mistakes. Surely a child could not be a mistake, no matter how it came into the world. Unable to articulate her feelings aloud, Morgana's body began to convulse, and she sobbed uncontrollably.

Grandmother's countenance softened. She moved closer and held Morgana and Lilian as one in a tight embrace. The years of distance between them disappeared with the tears, and the old bond between them was restored. Grandmother led Morgana to a seat by the fire and tenderly relieved her of the baby.

"She's a fairhead just like you were…"

Grandmother beamed and fretted over Lilian as she fixed her blanket and pulled the sleeping babe in close to her chest. Memories from the days before the death of her only child filled her, and she yearned to have such happiness again. Grandmother knew she could love the baby as if it were her own flesh and blood, as if it were Gorlois himself, but she also knew that she could not let her desires cloud her judgment. She needed to understand Morgana's plight more fully.

"Do not fret, my bellibone," she said to Morgana, using a pet name from the past. "Now, tell me the whole story."

Morgana told of Roselyn's scandalous coming

to the nunnery and how the two became fast friends. She shared everything she knew about Roselyn's hopes for the baby—a carefree childhood, a Christian upbringing, love, marriage. Grandmother listened attentively, nodding and frowning and lamenting in turn, but she gave the ears of her heart to Lilian. The baby's gentle breathing, the rising and falling of her chest, and the occasional wimper tugged at Grandmother and drowned out thought of all else but a second motherhood. It was only when Morgana described the involvement of the old spinster that Grandmother looked up.

"You say this woman has ill-repute. What exactly is it that people say about her?" Already, she feared the answer.

"Well...you know how people talk. They say, they say she is a witch," Morgana responded hesitantly. She did not want to admit that she believed it was true. She felt so unsure of the day's events that she could not be certain of her own actions, let alone the old spinster's. Had she been under a type of spell, or had she acted freely? She would leave that question for another time.

Grandmother looked Morgana straight in the eyes and asked, "Do you believe she acted in good faith to help Roselyn?"

"I am not sure what to think, Grandmother," Morgana answered honestly, shrugging her shoulders. "But, I doubt Lilian would be alive right now if it were not for her. No matter what her repute, the old spinster brought Roselyn's daughter safely into the world and provided for our journey hither."

Perhaps Morgana was right. Grandmother nodded in acquiescence and gazed at Lilian. She was unwilling to part with the baby, even if the spinster was the same woman whom she feared. She would worry about that another day. "Surely another bit of bobtale to keep the novices close to the convent," Grandmother hoped.

As the early morning light began to streak across the cottage through the cracks in the walls and shutters, the women formalized their pact. Grandmother agreed to take Lilian in—but only on condition Morgana return to the nunnery to finish her studies.

"Grandmother!" Morgana protested. "Do not ask me to go back and tarry there another day, let alone five more years! I could not endure it!"

"Bellibone, I know it will be hard for you, but you must not throw your life away in this endeavor." Grandmother swept her hand over Lilian as she spoke. "However meaningful it may be, it will keep you from living a life of your own, a life in the royal court with a husband and children someday."

"But this *would be* a life of my choosing. The nunnery is not!" Morgana declared forcefully.

"Yes, the nunnery was chosen for you…by your mother, the queen." A look of disdain crossed Grandmother's face at the mention of her daughter-in-law. "No matter what Igraine's indiscretions may be, she is your mother. You must respect her wishes." Glancing at the tapestry of the Garden of Eden, she continued resolutely, "Disobedience is the source of all vice and leads to perdition."

Morgana was incensed. "How can you, of all people, possibly desire me to obey my mother? She, who married the very man who killed your son, my father, before his body was cold in the grave, deserves no such respect!"

Her words cut deeply, but Grandmother was strong in her resolve. Though she knew Morgana had suffered greatly since the loss of her father, Grandmother could not indulge her foolhardiness. She believed going back to the nunnery would be good for her granddaughter. She hoped it would give her a greater sense of direction and an ability to finally deal with her grief. She worried, too, that Morgana was heading down a dangerous path of stubborn, self-righteousness. A mysterious disappearance would assuredly cast her deeper into the shadows and make her prey to vice.

"In my own time, I was not pleased to study at the nunnery, but it was the right thing in the end. You may not see it this way now, but it will be good for you, as it was good for me," Grandmother said as lovingly as possible. "Have faith."

Faith!

That was a word for the blind and submissive— surely not for Morgana, but she had no other choice but to accept Grandmother's terms.

"What shall I tell them of Roselyn and the baby?" Morgana questioned in a deflated voice. She knew further opposition was useless.

"Tell them the truth, or nearly the truth. Tell them Roselyn and the baby died in childbirth. Let them know the old spinster helped in the delivery. The nuns may not fully believe you, but they will certainly not go snooping around the spinster's cottage to check the facts if she is as feared as you say. Besides, you are royalty," Grandmother added snidely. "At least your mother's remarriage has brought you some advantages."

Morgana nodded obediently, her fiery spirit quelled for the time being.

"When your schooling is done, you will be free of all ties and able to join me hither if you so choose, though I doubt my humble cosh of a cottage will still suit your fancy. Until then, I will call for you as frequently as an old woman may without interrupting your studies." After a slight pause, Grandmother added, "But, I prithee, stay away from the old spinster. Further contact with her could be dangerous."

"Yes, Grandmother," Morgana agreed half-heartedly. Her lack of conviction was apparent, but the pact was sealed.

Grandmother smiled with satisfaction. "Your father would be proud. Now for some bellytimber. We need to put some meat on those bones of yours and bring out your figure, be you in a convent or not."

Morgana ate more than she wanted, but the poached eggs and leek porry were without taste. She had hoped seeing her grandmother would be a second chance for *her*, a way to cast off the cords that fastened round her heart. Instead, she felt bound with responsibility to others—to Roselyn, to Lilian, to her grandmother, and now even to her own mother. She thought about her father and wondered if he would be proud.

4

Days at the nunnery were more tolerable after Morgana's return despite the cloud of suspicion that hung around her. Just as her grandmother had predicted, Mother Superior accepted Morgana's explanation because she had to. The other novices, whom Morgana had never cared for in the first place, kept their distance. It was just as well. She had more space to do as she pleased that way. Only during her solitary walks to the market would she acknowledge how lonely she was and how much she longed for friendship.

On one such afternoon, Morgana set out with empty basket in hand. She shifted it awkwardly from one arm to another until she labored to carry it with both. Strong though she was, she had little energy for the outing and shrunk under the weight of the barren wicker.

Everywhere she looked reminded her of death. The trees were losing their leaves; the once plush grass now crackled under her feet; and the sky looked unusually bleak for an early morning in the Fall. She heard geese flying in companionship overhead, mocking her loneliness, and followed their flight with her eyes. Their path crossed directly above the old spinster's cottage.

Often had she thought of venturing back to that dreadful place. When she lay abed, unable to drift off to sleep, her mind would invent the most fantastic scenes. At times she would play the part of the brave heroine, standing off against the old spinster in a battle of wits and demanding answers about who she *really* was.

Tell me everything or else….

Then Morgana would realize she had no recourse nor power to do much of anything on her own. That was when she would turn to desperate pleas.

I am begging you…

Sometimes the old spinster would look kindly on Morgana and pity her plight by offering wisdom and understanding and even refuge. But always, the scene would end with the shrill sound of the spinster cackling and Morgana running for her life.

The torrent of images was too much for her as she walked to the market. Had the sky looked brighter or the grass felt softer that day, she may have kept her promise to her grandmother, but that was not to be. Morgana changed course, suddenly full of vigor, and marched right up to the little cottage with the basket swinging in step with her pace.

"I must," Morgana said to herself when she reached the threshold. She raised her fist and pounded on the door. The hard-knuckled sound was louder than she expected, but it was just what she needed to maintain her resolve. Morgana set her teeth and pounded again.

The door eased open, again, as if on its own. But this time, the rocking chair sat empty and motionless. Instead, the spinster stood next to a table set with a tea kettle and two earthen mugs. She wore a simple gown of dark linen. Though worn, it must have been a costly material. A belt threaded with golden silk wrapped around her waist and provided the only adornment to her person. Behind the haggard lines of her gaunt face was a faint hint of beauty, a trace of a former life. Her eyes were dark as an anvil and just as forceful.

"Just in time for tea," the old spinster said in a hoarse voice. Then coughing, she added, "Do you take milk and sugar?"

Morgana wanted to decline, but it was too late. The pretense of a formal social engagement made her fiery entry seem rudely out of place. She smoothed the folds of her skirt, straightened herself upright, and replied instead, "I do not mean to intrude, but I was hoping you might permit me to speak with you about the events surrounding my friend's death."

"Yes, I know why you have come hither," the spinster said in response. "Cream and sugar?" she asked again. Both mugs were now full of hot water and tea leaves, and the spinster prepared to add a spoonful of sugar to the mug intended for Morgana.

"Black," Morgana pronounced, though she had

never previously taken her tea that way.

Raising her eyebrows, the spinster set the sugar aside and motioned for Morgana to sit. "We have not been formally introduced. My name is Eloise, though few use my Christian name these days and prefer the most loathsome of epithets."

Morgana flushed.

"You, of course, are Morgana le Fay, daughter of the queen."

"Yes," Morgana said cautiously as she took a seat and clasped her hands around the hot mug. "How is it you know so much about me?"

Eloise gave a slight chuckle. "I have eyes and ears all about the Realm of Logres. They reveal what I need to know."

"Does that mean you need to know about me?" Morgana asked a little more boldly. Her sense of caution was overcome by curiosity.

"You have been chosen for a special quest, one that will impact the entire Realm of Logres. So, yes, you could say I *need* to know about you." The words seeped from Eloise's mouth full of meaning and mystery, drawing Morgana more deeply into the conversation.

"What is my quest?" Morgana asked incredulously. Her eyes narrowed on Eloise, and she braced herself for the response.

Eloise took a deep breath of her steamy mug and flared her nostrils like a dragon. "You must learn that on your own, and, indeed, you will. In the meantime, I will provide instruction in the arts you will need to be successful."

"Arts? What kind of arts do I need?"

Eloise sipped the tea and licked her lips. "Arts that good Christian women shy away from for fear of being in control of their own destiny. You would like that, would you not, Morgana? To be in control of your own destiny instead of being forced to comply with the will of others."

Eloise's words at once repelled and attracted Morgana. Unsure of the best response, she spoke honestly. "I do not know what I want. I came hither to ask about Roselyn's death and how you had prepared for my departure with Lilian. I did not come hither to take on a quest."

"Such are the twists and turns of Fate—when you do not have control," Eloise retorted after a long draught. "We need not discuss the matter further. If you want answers, you will be given them—in good time. For now, rest assured that Roselyn's death was predetermined. I did everything in my power to make it comfortable. Lilian's fate, on the other hand, is not yet set in stone. Much depends on you."

"What do you mean?" Morgana asked. "She is now in the care of my grandmother, as you must know, and I have not even seen her these many months."

"But you will, come Michaelmas and for many a feast day after that," Eloise replied knowingly. "When you helped bring the child into the world, you bound her life to your own and unwittingly accepted the quest I spoke of. She will live or die according to your actions, and such will determine the fate of Logres." She paused to let the words take effect.

Morgana was listening with great intent. "Prithee, go on," she urged. Her interest was piqued as much out of her newfound self-worth as it was for the sake of helping Lilian. She was thrilled by the notion that the fate of her step-father's kingdom was somehow in her hands.

"Your quest will satisfy that which you want most. I am here to offer tutelage…if you so desire it. Your path is set in motion either way. With my help you will be successful. Without it, well, that is for you to discover."

The women sat in silence with Morgana peering into her untouched tea and Eloise preparing herself a second cup. So they would have remained if a blood-curdling hiss had not disturbed them. It was the cat. She had slunk into the room unnoticed, spotted a mouse, and trapped it in her paws.

Morgana nearly jumped out of her seat at the sound. She fumbled for a moment, curtsied awkwardly, and tried to act natural. "Grammarcy for your hospitality. I better be on my way."

Eloise smiled at Morgana's pretense of formality and responded in kind. "Yes, you best not be too far behind the other novices. It was so kind of you to visit. I look forward to seeing you again soon."

Morgana knew Eloise spoke truly. As the door closed behind her, the urge to go back already consumed her.

5

Once the nunnery was in sight, Morgana noticed a royal carriage in wait at the stables, a most unusual occurrence. The insignia of the House of Pendragon was blazed on its side, and a footman stood feeding the noble steeds. Morgana looked at her empty basket and flushed for shame. While she usually managed to avoid the watchful eyes of the other women, she worried this unannounced visit, which was surely on her account, would bring her under even greater suspicion and perhaps garner a scolding. That was the last thing she needed reported back to her step-father.

Scanning the fields, Morgana spotted a section with ample wild flowers and hurriedly gathered them into her basket. At least she would no longer be empty-handed. Besides, she could claim to have spent the day "contemplating God's beauteous creation" instead of going to the market. Morgana smirked at her cunning.

"Ah, there you are, Morgana," Mother Superior cooed when Morgana passed through the main doors. A strained smile stretched across her face, but it was not for the sake of the regal entourage. It was for the pain she felt on Morgana's behalf.

"The royal house sent a courier this morrow, shortly after you left for the market, to inform us of your mother's impending visit. We tried to bring you back early to ready yourself but failed."

Morgana straightened herself upright in preparation for her planned response, but Mother Superior kept going. Either she did not notice the contents of her basket, or she was overlooking it for some unknown reason. Morgana's mind flashed back to the day she learned of her father's death. She had soiled a new dress playing in the river, and her mother had uncharacteristically ignored her appearance *and* the wasted money.

Something is wrong…

"The queen arrived just before you. She is in the chapel and requests your presence," Mother Superior explained as she hurriedly escorted Morgana through the narrow halls that led to the chapel, motioned for her to enter, and then slipped away without a sound.

The spacious room was deadly quiet, oppressive, and foreboding. Late afternoon sunlight streaked through the stained-glass lancet windows that lined each side of the pews leading up to the altar. Images of the saints seemed to taunt Morgana, who felt particularly out of place in the presence of the tabernacle. She stole a glimpse at the statue of the Blessed Mother and then lowered her eyes. Her own mother kneeled reverently before the cross.

She was dressed in black with a veil of the same color covering her face.

Morgana approached her and ventured to break the silence, but words would not come. There was no need, however. Her mother, as always, was in full command of the meeting. She slowly reclined in the pew and folded her hands on her lap. "The king is dead. Pack your things so we can return to our demesne in Wales. We must hurry."

Morgana should have rejoiced at the news, but she was incensed. Anger flooded her heart at the thought she would be denied vengeance on Uther—the king, her step-father, the man who had killed her father. She could only mutter a single word.

"How?"

"Likely poisoned. The king took supper in his chambers on Tuesday night and then turned in early. He was feeling ill and thought it was simply indigestion. However, he awoke fevered and in a cold sweat. We summoned the leecher but to little avail. Two more nights he lay in bed, tormented with pain, until death claimed him," the queen concluded.

"Mother, I am not sorry to hear of his death. Little love did I have for him, as you well know. I am sorry for your loss, though. May God take pity on *you*," Morgana replied icily. The dual meaning of her words was clear. "What of my half-brother?"

"Has your time in hither convent taught you compassion? Or are you still reeling in unfounded jealousy?" the queen scoured. "If you must know, Arthur is safely hidden where no one will be able to do him harm. Now, I prithee, put the past behind you and gather your things at once. We may all be in danger."

"No, Mother," Morgana replied unexpectedly. Her words were flat but strong. "I intend to finish my studies here. The nunnery may not feel like home, but it is more of one than the old manor house could possibly be without father." She hesitated a moment, relishing the blow she struck. At least the sting meant Mother had *some* feelings left within her.

Morgana continued, "I believe I have been called hither. I am not sure to what or why, but I think there is more for me at the convent than I realized at first. You were right in sending me to this place."

The queen stared at Morgana as she considered a reply. They had never been close. Even as a baby, Morgana had preferred her father, and that had been a source of bitter disappointment for the queen. Igraine had imagined motherhood as an experience of shared love. Instead, her attempts at kindling a bond with her only daughter had been unrequited. It was not that Morgana had meant to slight her mother, of course. In her youthful self-centeredness, she was altogether unaware that her preference for her father was so hurtful to her mother. But the slights, though naïve enough at first, turned into a full-fledged assault when Gorlois died and Igraine married his assassin. As a practical woman, Igraine had seen no reason not to marry Uther Pendragon and ensure the future of her family. Besides, the marriage had been as much for Morgana's well-being as her own. How foolish she had been to think her daughter would have been able to see that. But now, in the small, dimly lit chapel, Igraine wondered if Morgana was finally growing up. Perhaps she *was* benefiting from the nunnery as Uther had insisted, but to what avail? Their future was once again uncertain. Surely the nunnery would be no less safe than their manor in Wales.

Igraine sighed. "Morgana, I will not compel you to leave against your will. Happy I am that you feel called hither to a house of the Lord. God grant you the grace to accept His will and serve Him faithfully." The queen's arms ached to hold her daughter, but Morgana gave no invitation to do so. "I will have your room made ready should you change your mind."

With that, the queen genuflected deeply before the altar and left.

Wait…

But Morgana could not humble herself enough to call out and show her mother even the slightest sign of love or respect. Well she knew she may regret the lost opportunity to leave the nunnery, but her mind was fixed on the quest of which Eloise spoke. The new development of Uther's death made her all the more eager to seek the spinster's counsel. Morgana was perplexed. She had been promised that which she hoped most, but surely that could not be since the object of her vengeance was already dead. She needed answers and was unwilling to find them out during the natural course of time.

Even the week she would have to wait for the next market day felt unbearable.

Morgana set out early on the following Saturday to meet Eloise. A strange familiarity had already grown between them as a result of their last meeting, and Morgana let herself in after only a quick rap on the door. Again, two cups of steaming tea were set at the table. The only difference was that Morgana's cup had already been prepared with cream and sugar. Clasping the mug in her hand, Morgana allowed herself to take a tentative sip of the strong brew. It had a sweet, comforting taste reminiscent of her childhood happiness. Morgana recoiled at the thought of mixing the two worlds: one so good and wholesome, the other so dark and mysterious.

She set the mug down and jumped right into the conversation. "If you want me to accept your tutelage, then you must tell me more. I will not blindly walk this path with you."

"You are wise to inquire so, although you may not be fully satisfied with my answers. There is but little I can share before the events unfold, for too much knowledge of the future risks changing it, and the consequences of which could be disastrous. I can, however, tell you Lilian's life will be threatened three times. The first threat will be on her fifth birthday. The second will be on her thirteenth, and the third will be on her sixteenth. You will hold the power of life and death in your hands at each turn."

"And what of the Realm of Logres?" Morgana questioned impatiently. "My step-father, the king, is dead, as you must certainly know. How can any of this be connected to him?"

"Oh, Child," Eloise began, "you have much to learn. Your vision is far too narrow. His house may seem to have fallen, but it is merely lying in wait."

Morgana suddenly saw her half-brother, Arthur, before her eyes and recalled the only time she had ever held him in her arms. He had been shrieking unbearably, and the nanny was away from the nursery. Morgana picked him up, desperate for peace and quiet. A foul smell instantly filled her nostrils, and warm curdled moosh smeared across her dress. Morgana thundered in disgust, drawing the nanny back in a frazzle. The nanny near fell over with laugher when she saw the stinky mess and realized why Morgana was so upset.

"You will have your revenge, if you so desire it, but not without paying a heavy price," Eloise continued.

"What price? I must know," Morgana demanded.

"It is still too early for me to tell you, but time will reveal all. Rest assured, the fate of the House of Pendragon is in your hands as surely as the life of Lilian."

As Morgana pondered Eloise's words, the faint voices of her father and grandmother began calling out to her, growing louder and louder, crowding her mind. Were they telling her to retreat or charge forward? It was too noisy. She shook her head and tried to make out what they were saying, but she could not. Desperate for relief, she pulled the mug to her lips, took a drink, and quelled the voices. Her eyes rested on the sweet brew. In the silence of her mind, she heard her own small whisper, her own urge and desire.

"Teach me what I need to know."

"As you wish. But," Eloise raised a spindly finger, "beware none learn of your powers. You must work in absolute secrecy or else threaten the success of your mission. The world must see you as a regular maiden, not a sorceress."

And so began Morgana's instruction in the black arts. Many a wintry afternoon did she set out for the spinster's under the pretense of taking a prayerful walk through nature. Really she was practicing the spells Eloise required her to memorize, full of words that unlocked the powers of nature itself and placed them in Morgana's fair hands. Over and over again, she turned them until she wore them like a glove.

Mother Superior initially doubted Morgana's purpose in her "nature walks," but so deft did Morgana become at living a double life that not even Mother Superior suspected what Morgana was actually up to. At Eloise's bidding, Morgana embraced her studies at the convent and squelched the intense scrutiny she had been under. Morgana convinced everyone, including herself, into believing she was leading a virtuous life.

PART II

The Water's Edge

The heavy sleep within my head was smashed
by an enormous thunderclap, so that
I started up as one whom force awakens;
I stood erect and turned my rested eyes
from side to side, and I stared steadily
to learn what place it was surrounding me.
In truth, I found myself upon the brink
of an abyss, the melancholy valley
containing thundering, unending wailings.

- DANTE ALIGHIERI, *THE DIVINE COMEDY*,
CANTO IV, VERSES 1-9

1

Morgana awoke with a start. For nearly five years, she had been dreading the anniversary of Roselyn's death as the day that would herald the first threat on Lilian's life. She now had but one day left of her countdown, one day more before her own fortitude and abilities would be tested. Everything had been carefully arranged according to Eloise's instruction. Morgana would visit Grandmother and Lilian unexpectedly as a "birthday surprise." She would gain Mother Superior's permission for the trip under the pretext she was needed to assist with the Spring planting. Indeed, Mother Superior, who knew nothing of Lilian's existence, had come to admire Morgana's devotion to her grandmother and would permit her to visit during every major holiday and for many special circumstances such as this one. A carriage for the day's journey was provided and already waiting at the stables.

Morgana dressed quickly and gathered the small parcel she arranged the night before, packed with fresh undergarments, a simple linen gown, a comb, and a smooth black toadstone. Looking around the sparse room, she wondered how she had managed to get by on so little for so long.

Morgana left her room just as the bells announcing prime began to toll. Dozens of women poured quietly out of their rooms and made their way to the chapel. Looking into the sea of black habits, it was not hard to discern who would take final vows, who would simply reside at the convent for study, and who, like herself and Roselyn, had been compelled to join the nunnery as a form of penance. Morgana could not help but wonder if any of the women would experience a twist of fate like her own. Heavy with the quest before her, Morgana closed her cell door and headed to the stables.

When, after several long hours, the carriage drove down the road leading up to Grandmother's cottage, Morgana began to scan the terrain. Sure enough, her eyes lighted on a small, familiar figure. Two small legs sprang from the woods and ran in a child-like attempt to catch up to the fast-paced carriage. Morgana slowed the carriage to a gentle trot, and Lilian managed to playfully run at its side, laughing and skipping along every few steps in eager anticipation. The child's golden-brown hair shone in the afternoon sun as it flounced down her back.

"Grandmother! Grandmother!" Lilian called out as she ran. "Aunty Morgana is here! Aunty Morgana is here!"

Morgana smiled at the girl's sweetness and longed for the carefree days of her own childhood. If only life were still so simple! She reigned in the horses, stepped down from the carriage, and held out her arms to the bounding child.

"My, how you have grown!" she said. Then with the deliberate affection adults use when talking to young children, she asked, "How old are you now?"

"I turn five on the morrow!" Lilian exclaimed, clapping her hands and jumping up and down. "Grandmother is baking a special cake. Will you stay?"

"I would love to celebrate with you, not to mention eat Grandma's delicious cake. What great luck for me that I will get to enjoy both!" Morgana responded playfully.

Grandmother looked on from the doorway and waited for Lilian to take a breath. "Lilian, where are your manners? We must always welcome our guests indoors as soon as they arrive and not prattle on so. We do not want to be thought rude; now do we?"

Lilian smiled at Grandmother's mock scolding. She had come to expect such reprimands from her grandmother as an expression of love, as a way of teaching her goodness. Grandmother did not have the heart to truly scold Lilian, nor did she have the need. Lilian was a dutifully obedient child.

Once evening settled in and Lilian was shooed off to bed, Grandmother inquired about Morgana's unannounced visit. "Lilian was thrilled to see you today. Grammarcy for making a special trip, which I presume is in honor of her birthday." Truly, Grandmother, who had a type of sixth sense, felt something was amiss.

Morgana simply smiled in response.

Still persistent, Grandmother added as if an afterthought, "We were not expecting you until Paschalmas."

"I only received formal permission for this trip in the last few days, so I did not have time to write," replied Morgana. "Besides, I thought it would be a nice birthday surprise." Though she attempted to sound casual, she did not.

How tired Morgana was of playing these games with her grandmother. Perhaps she should just tell her everything. Morgana's eyes wandered to the tapestry of the Garden of Eden, and she thought better of it. Grandmother was too morally upright to understand the virtue in the necessity of her plight to save Lilian.

Grandmother sensed Morgana was holding back. "Is everything okay, Bellibone? You seem burdened with thought."

Composure is everything.

Morgana should have been grateful for the question, but she felt annoyed instead. She was annoyed first at her grandmother for asking and second at herself for being unable to hide her distress. The plan was to behave like normal. Such was essential if Morgana was to succeed in averting the threat on Lilian's life, and Morgana was now painfully aware that her emotions showed. Eloise would be so disappointed.

Mind you act natural.

"You worry too much, Grandmother," Morgana

replied hastily. "I am fine. If I seem a little out of sorts, it is from thinking of Roselyn. Lilian's birth, joyful as it may be to you and her, is a very sad day for me as it marks the death of my dear friend."

Her explanation was sufficient. Grandmother felt reassured that Morgana was indeed fine. She put aside her worries, and the women began to speak freely about all manner of things. They talked about Morgana's mother, who had remarried yet again. Though a favorable match, it was none to Morgana's nor Grandmother's liking. They talked about the state of the kingdom and reluctantly conceded that it had not been on steady footing since the death of Uther Pendragon. Feudal rivalry and bloodshed was at an all-time high with no respite in sight. Even after nearly five years, Logres had not crowned a new king, so the lords ruled their manors at the point of a sword, and the heathen Saxons were gaining more and more ground in Britain.

After having had their fill of bitter conversation, the women broached the lighter subject of plans for the morrow.

"Lilian wants to picnic by the river, so we will go there after she finishes her chores and lessons for the day," Grandmother said. "I suspect we will remain thither for much of the afternoon. She loves playing by the water, just like you used to."

Morgana smiled at the comparison. She liked the idea she and Lilian shared things in common. "Are there no other plans for the morrow?"

It was imperative Morgana know precisely what

to expect in order to prepare for the long anticipated threat on Lilian's life. Eloise had never revealed the nature of the peril, just the day on which it would occur. This foreknowledge had always seemed like plenty of information to permit Morgana to save Lilian. But now on the eve of the threat, it seemed like almost nothing to go by. Anything could happen during the twenty-four-hour window, and Morgana knew she needed to gather as much information about the events of the day as possible to try to pinpoint potential dangers.

"Not unless Lilian changes her mind, which I doubt. She has been talking about picnicking for weeks now. With your arrival, I suspect she will be all the more eager to go. She has built quite the sanctuary for herself by the river, and she will no doubt want to show it all to you," Grandmother replied, rising from her chair. "We best turn in. The hour is late, and we will need our strength tomorrow."

How truly you speak…

Sleep could not come fast enough for Morgana who was weary in mind and body. No sooner did her eyes close shut, then thunder crackled outside, warning of a storm.

2

Morgana sat up in bed surprisingly refreshed from the night's rest. Stretching, she looked outside the window and saw it had rained. It must have been a heavy downpour because water pooled in sections throughout the uneven terrain. Though the birds could be heard singing in the trees, the other animals were still in hiding, and a gentle stillness pervaded the area like that only found in the aftermath of a storm. Despite her natural cynicism, Morgana could not help but take the beautiful morning as a good omen.

The smell of bacon wafted up to her room and bade Morgana greet the day with enthusiasm. She smiled as she dressed and even hummed along with the birds. Just as she opened the door to leave, her eyes flashed upon the crucifix hanging on the wall. Light from the morning sun reflected off the beautifully crafted bronze icon, and Morgana felt a momentary sense of reverence. Perhaps it was simply out of habit from time spent at the convent, but Morgana bowed her head slightly before grabbing the toadstone from her bag. It looked like nothing more than a sleek round pebble, the likes of which were used for all manner of medicinal purposes, but it was actually a talisman Eloise had entrusted in her care. Morgana had grown accustomed to holding it when casting a spell. It gave her strength.

Grandmother greeted Morgana with a cheerful, "Good morrow!" and then busily continued with her preparations for breakfast. Meanwhile, Lilian was sitting in the corner with a large illuminated Bible on her lap and was deep in study. Her lips were moving, but hardly a sound could be heard except when she would ask Grandmother for help with a word. Though young, Lilian could already read quite well, thanks not only to her eagerness to learn but also to Grandmother's persistent instruction.

"The ability to read and write is a virtue in itself," Grandmother would say. "It will strengthen your mind and help you build the discipline needed to be a good Christian."

For that reason, Lilian spent every morning reading from the Bible and patiently copying its endless passages. She received little other formal instruction. Instead, like most girls, Lilian learned the necessities of keeping house—sewing, spinning, cooking—by simply watching and helping her grandmother. Lilian enjoyed these tasks immensely. She took pleasure in the act of creating and, even at her young age, desired to make things beautiful. How different Lilian was from Morgana. When the latter was a child, she refused to sit for her lessons, always preferring instead to run about and play.

Morgana looked on in wonder. Lilian was an unusually gifted child with a promising life before her. If only Fate was not always lurking in the shadows, threatening to pluck Lilian's life as it had done her mother's. Morgana tensed at the thought of the portending danger and compulsively clenched and unclenched her fists, cracking her knuckles as she did so. Then, very slowly, she smoothed out the folds of her skirt, brushing her left hand across the talisman. Feeling once again in control of the day, Morgana ventured to chat with her grandmother.

"May I help you get breakfast ready?" Morgana offered. She was determined to maintain her composure in the face of the day's mounting pressures.

"Belibonne," Grandmother replied with her characteristic mock scolding, "that would have been a very nice gesture an hour ago, or even ten minutes ago when you finally came down. I thought Mother Superior required you to awake at dawn?"

Without another word, Morgana went to the pantry, collected three bowls and spoons, and began setting the table.

"Now you are crowding me out of my own kitchen," Grandmother protested with a wry smile on her lips. Then, giving a nod, she added, "At least you are making yourself useful."

And so after a few more preparations, Lilian was called to the table, and breakfast was served with a heavy dose of birthday fanfare.

It felt like a long morning. Morgana anxiously kept herself busy while keeping a constant eye on

Lilian. Morgana hurried from one chore to the next, clearing the table, washing the dishes, scattering feed for the animals, and so on, until there seemed little else to do. Lilian was just as eager to finish her chores, so when the time came for her to practice needlepoint, she carelessly pricked her thumb, which was something she had never done before. Dark red blood seeped into the canvas, discoloring the otherwise immaculate stitches. Lilian was so distraught at the mistake, tears welled up in her eyes.

"Never mind a little imperfection," Morgana said comfortingly, as she took the needlework in her hands. "It makes your work more interesting."

"But I was nearly done, and this section will be almost impossible to take out and stitch again," Lilian replied, her face flush with emotion.

"It looks beauteous still," Morgana reassured her. "In fact, I think it is more so to have imperfections like this because such is the way of life. Art should reflect life the way it is, not as we would have it."

Morgana could not tell if Lilian understood her meaning, but the child seemed satisfied with the explanation. Her warm cheeks cooled, Lilian resumed the last section of stitching. She worked more carefully than before, no longer intent on finishing but on the process of creating beauty.

As Morgana went back to keeping herself busy with mindless tasks around the cottage, she continued to keep an eye on Lilian. She noticed a serenity about the child. It seemed as if a soft glow radiated around her. So peaceful was she in her work, that Morgana felt more at peace herself. It was hard to imagine the day ushering in tragedy, but she knew it must be so. By now, she was certain the long-foretold threat would surface at the waterside. She could envision no other scenario in which Lilian would be in danger.

3

When the hour finally arrived to picnic by the river, Lilian bounced about gleefully. She ran ahead and circled back to Morgana and Grandmother every few hundred feet. The back and forth made Morgana uncomfortable, and she kept beckoning Lilian to stay within reach.

"Do not fret so," Grandmother said to Morgana. "You ran about just as independently as Lilian does, and you were fine. It is good for a child to run free."

Morgana sighed in response. "I suppose you are right." But inwardly, she hoped Grandmother would not regret her words. Placing her hand in her pocket, Morgana rolled her fingers around the talisman.

They settled into a lively spot by the river. The water was higher and faster than usual because of the previous night's storm, and the earth was still wet and muddy by the edge. The birds were noisy overhead, perched high in the trees, and several squirrels and bunnies hovered in hopes of snagging a morsel to eat.

After Grandmother spread a blanket on the wet

earth, she began laying out the contents of her heavy basket with an added ceremonial flare. Lilian squealed in delight. Grandmother had prepared fresh bread with honey butter, mincemeat pie, custard, and, of course, her delicious spiced cake with currants. It was a feast the likes of which Lilian had never seen before, and it was all in her honor. Grandmother had gone to great lengths to make the day a memorable one, and, indeed, it would be, though for quite a different reason than either she or Lilian could have imagined.

Once all was laid out, Grandmother led their small party in a blessing. Then Grandmother revealed yet another surprise. She reached into her basket and pulled out a small, yellow, silk bundle. Handing it to Lilian, she said simply, "Happy birthday, Love."

Lilian spread the folds open and gasped. The insides revealed a gold crucifix strung across a heavy embroidery cord.

"Grammarcy, Grandmother!" Lilian oozed in a hushed voice, reflecting not only her gratitude and surprise, but also a deep reverence for the gift itself.

"May God grace you with His love today and always. Turn around," Grandmother ordered so she could tie the necklace about Lilian's neck. Once it was securely knotted, she said, "Now, let us enjoy the meal before us."

Grandmother feasted mostly with her eyes, just as a lady should, but forced food on her companions like a hostess must. Lilian focused on the custard and spiced cake, but Morgana tried everything so as not to disappoint Grandmother. She ate herself into such a warm, languid state that she groaned when Lilian ran off and only reluctantly ventured to get up and follow her.

"Let her play for now," Grandmother said with a soft touch on Morgana's arm. "I was hoping you would say a Rosary with me in offering for the repose of Roselyn's soul." Grandmother hesitated. "You were right last night to remind me of her. In my happiness at having Lilian to care for, I have selfishly ignored the obvious loss of her mother."

Morgana froze. She was anxious to follow after Lilian, but something was holding her to the ground and compelling her to stay. She could hear a faint voice in her head.

You must rest in me. The child will be fine.

She so longed to heed its words, tired as she suddenly felt from the food, the outing, the day, the quest. Yet, at the same time, the face of Eloise appeared before her, coldly staring Morgana in the eyes, urging her to set forth and remain vigilant.

Get up. The hour is at hand.

Morgana felt all the pressure of her double-life rise to the surface. Her mind swirled as she struggled over what to do. She reached for her pocket, but Grandmother deftly placed a set of Rosary beads in her hands before she could grab the talisman. The smooth feel of the beads calmed Morgana, and without another word, the women began to say in unison, "In the Name of the Father, and the Son, and the Holy Ghost…"

Hardly fifteen minutes had passed before the Rosary was concluded. Morgana awoke from her slumber-like prayer and felt suddenly anxious once more to find Lilian. Just as she was excusing herself, the two women heard a loud cracking noise accompanied by a piercing scream.

Morgana's nimble legs carried her as fast as they could in the direction of the noise. She turned the pages of Eloise's spell book in her mind, pulled out the talisman from her pocket, and chanted lowly:

Grasses glide me, hard earth anchor,
Swift and steady, to my legs take her.

The ground beneath her feet was a slippery sludge of mud, but Morgana's powers made her stride quick and sure, like a wild animal on the hunt. With each step, she gained more poise, drawing from nature's invisible energy. She continued:

Shadows shorten, daylight linger,
Brilliant rays, to my eyes bring her.

The scant daylight brightened, and Morgana's eyes rested on a solitary tree growing out from the bank. Its bark was of a dark, greenish brown, and its barren branches confirmed it was dead. Nevertheless, the tree shivered in the setting sun, as if it was trying to say something to Morgana. Drawing still greater power, she called forth:

Arbor waken, timber whisker,
Lilian's danger, to my ears whisper.

Suddenly, a rotten tree limb, ugly with age and deformity, burst forth from the rocks with a splash and revealed beautiful golden-brown locks swirling furiously just beneath the surface. Lilian's small body floated unresponsively under the water. Morgana bounded from rock to rock and chanted:

Mighty rocks, rushing river,
Strong and gentle, to my arms bring her.

Flooded with strength, Morgana heaved the heavy limb out of the way and sunk her arms deep into the water. With a swift, gentle tug, she lifted the girl's limp body and dragged her to the shore. She knelt over the child and breathed deeply into her lungs. After a few compressions on her chest, Lilian spewed murky water out of her mouth and began coughing and crying. She would live.

"Praise God Almighty!" Grandmother cried out, falling down on her knees beside Morgana and Lilian and gasping for breath herself. Despite her strength for a woman her age, Grandmother was sorely winded. She had not been able to keep up with Morgana and had only arrived in time to see Lilian's resuscitation from a short distance. She witnessed nothing of the supernatural powers behind Morgana's rescue. "Praise God Almighty!" she gasped again, as her chest heaved up and down.

Morgana looked at the pale child in her arms. Her color changed from chalky white to faded yellow, and a look of awareness began to creep in.

"I was climbing the tree…" Lilian coughed in confusion.

"Never mind what happened. You are safe now," Morgana replied quietly, looking into Lilian's deep, pleading eyes. The girl looked like a wounded animal. "You need fear nothing, Little One. As long as I live, I will always protect you."

Then, for the first time since her father's death, Morgana felt the warm trickle of tears fall down her cheeks.

4

The evening was somber. Grandmother put Lilian to bed early and said little to Morgana. Instead, she sat by the fire, took out her Rosary beads, and prayed. She wrapped so many decades around her fingers that they bled. Try as she did to meditate on the mysteries, she kept blaming herself for Lilian's close call with death. She blamed her age, her stubborn body, her carefree spirit, her divided attention. She thanked God that Morgana had been there but found herself blaming Morgana as well. She knew it was a shallow thought, a way to excuse herself, but Grandmother could not shake the notion that Morgana was somehow more wrapped up in the day's events than it appeared. Her mind jumped from memories of Morgana as a little girl, to those of her as a young woman, and then to her behavior over the last two days. Something was amiss, but Grandmother could not figure out what.

Morgana, on the other hand, felt a load had been lifted. After so many years of worrying and so many years of training under Eloise, she could at last take comfort in having succeeded in accomplishing her first quest. It was a good feeling. She withdrew for bed earlier than usual and settled into what she hoped would be a restful night of sleep. Much to her dismay, however, images of Lilian's lifeless body, face down in the water, tormented her whenever she closed her eyes. She tossed and turned in bed unable to shake the gruesome images and fall asleep. Frustrated, she finally sat up and stared blindly into the darkness. She needed something, anything, to focus on to get her mind off the horrible images, and her eyes reluctantly settled for the crucifix hanging on the wall directly in front of her bed. At first, she just stared coldly at the holy icon as if in a stupor. Then, something incredible happened. The crucifix began to put off a warm light, and a voice spoke out in a soft whisper.

Do not abandon me. I wait for you by the river.

No sooner were the holy words spoken, then the glow subsided. Morgana knew not what they meant, but she was wise enough to heed its command. She grabbed her robe and set out once more for the river with the moon overhead to show the way. The night was frantic with the rising and falling sound of crickets chirping, and Morgana caught its rhythm. She quickened and slackened her pace again and again to the insects' music. It carried her as if by force, never allowing her to catch her breath for more than a moment. She was sweating by the time she got to the river.

Morgana darted from one area to the next but

saw nothing out of the ordinary. "How silly I have been," she said aloud to herself. "As if a crucifix would speak to *me* of all people."

Feeling foolish, she turned to go back to the cottage, but then she realized all was quiet, deadly quiet. The crickets had stopped chirping. Their silence spoke danger. Something was out there, something she could feel down to the depths of her being. Morgana stretched her ears. It sounded like a small animal was climbing the rocks along the river bank. There was nothing unusual about that, of course, but Morgana could not ignore her supernatural instincts. Besides, she had not traveled all that way during the middle of the night to leave any suspicion uninvestigated. Drawing closer to the rocks, she was able to make out the noise more clearly. It was not an animal climbing but some other creature struggling to hold onto the rocks and avoid being sucked away by the current. Fear gripped Morgana as she realized the creature was Lilian.

"Hold on, Lilian!" Morgana ordered. "I am coming to get you."

Morgana reached for her talisman and groaned in disbelief when she discovered her pocket empty. Of all the things to forget! Panic set in. She stepped forward cautiously with arms outspread at her side. The rocks were slippery, and Morgana lost her balance and fell down hard on her knees. Pain pulsated throughout her body, and she dared not try to stand again. Still determined, she began crawling out along the rocks.

"I am almost there. Hold on!" Morgana called out in an attempt to calm herself as much as Lilian. Without the talisman, however, Morgana felt weak and scared. Words of enchantment echoed through her mind in an inarticulate jumble. Try as she did, she could not draw forth her powers.

Lilian meanwhile struggled to keep her head above the rushing current and inhaled the frothy mist with every breath. She could not last much longer, even if she managed to hold onto the slimy rock.

Powerless, Morgana feared not only for Lilian but for herself. She, too, was one false move away from getting washed away by the current. She would not give into her fear, though. She had to continue on no matter the outcome. Inch by inch, she crawled along the cold, slippery rocks, pausing every few seconds to calm her nerves and get her bearings. When she was no more than an arm's length away, she sought a place to grip her feet and legs and reached out to Lilian, who was barely clinging on.

"Take my hand," Morgana called out in a shaky voice.

Lilian attempted to disengage one of her hands, but she was too scared to let go. Morgana stretched even further and managed to get within inches of Lilian's position.

"You can do it. Reach!" Morgana commanded, but Lilian still would not budge. Desperate and afraid, Morgana screamed at the five-year-old, "Take my hand or you will die!"

Lilian looked terrified, but she obeyed. She lifted her hand and stretched it out. Morgana was not fast enough, however. No sooner did Lilian release one hand, then her other gave way, and she slid further back on the rock and begun to go under. As she did so, Morgana caught the glint of something woven between Lilian's submerged fingers. It was her newly gifted crucifix necklace, and it seemed to say in a garbled voice.

Do not abandon me!

The words sank deep down into Morgana's soul and drew forth a courage and strength she had only known from the talisman. With a sudden surge of confidence, Morgana slid across the rocks, grabbed Lilian by the arms, and pulled her out of the water. She held her close for a moment, and then instinctively led her one step at a time to the grassy shore.

Before either could catch her breath, Morgana demanded, "What were you thinking coming here in the middle of the night? Of all the foolish things!"

Lilian had never been scolded by anyone before. She broke down and sobbed uncontrollably. The day's events were simply too much for the little girl.

Thinking better of her approach, Morgana tried again more gently. "Oh, Love, please do not cry. You are safe now. You are safe…" She coddled and petted Lilian, told her not to worry, and said everything would be okay. Only after several minutes did Lilian begin to calm down.

"I lost my new crucifix when I fell in this afternoon, so I came hither to find it," Lilian fumbled to say between sobs. "I did not want to disappoint Grandmother."

"Dear, sweet, foolish child," was all Morgana could say as she swept Lilian up in her arms and carried her back to the cottage. The crickets rejoiced in hymn, and the moon smiled at the sight. Morgana realized it was about midnight. The first threat on Lilian's life had been prevented once and for all.

Grandmother was told of the late night misadventure on the following morn, though Morgana spared her the torment of knowing just how perilous the situation had been. Grandmother, still in a haze, was much too mentally and emotionally exhausted to ask questions.

As Morgana readied herself for the return trip to the convent, she noticed Lilian undoing her needle-work. "I thought you finished that project."

"The stain looked ugly. I am going to fix it," Lilian replied without looking up from the canvas. She was concentrating on every stitch with statue-like determination. Lilian would not allow herself to make another careless mistake.

Lilian's words stung. After all they had been through together! After all Morgana had done! How could Lilian so quickly dismiss her? Morgana had expected Lilian to show an undying gratitude. Instead, the young girl withdrew into her own world much like Grandmother had done. Of course, Lilian did not mean to hurt Morgana's feelings, but the damage was done, and it would leave a stain far more difficult to remove.

And so feeling rebuffed by the child for whom she had sacrificed so much, Morgana left with a short farewell. She directed the carriage to stop at Eloise's on the way to the convent. She longed for the reassurance that only one who knew of Morgana's quest could offer.

Before she even reached for the knob, the door swung open and Eloise greeted her with, "You have done well, Morgana. We have much to discuss, but first, you must rest."

Without thinking, Morgana blurted out, "But I have lost the talisman…"

"It was merely a black pebble, not even a toad-stone, I gave you to build your confidence. You never needed it to perform magic." Pulling Morgana into an embrace, she continued, "Be silent now and rest with the knowledge that you have been successful in the first part of your quest."

"So you know what happened…?" Morgana continued in a small voice.

"Everything," Eloise replied.

"Then what of the crucifix?" Morgana simply needed to know if God had spoken to her or if her powers had somehow manifest differently.

"Shhh. Everything was and still is in your hands," Eloise spoke half-truthfully. "You must rest now."

Such was just the encouragement Morgana needed. She had found her rightful place at last, even if Grandmother's hugs were better.

PART III

Amidst the Shadows

We began to make our way across
a wood on which no path had left its mark.
No green leaves in that forest, only black;
no branches straight and smooth, but knotted,
gnarled;
no fruits were there, but briers bearing poison.
Even those savage beasts that roam between
Cécina and Corneto, beasts that hate
tilled lands, do not have holts so harsh and dense.

- DANTE ALIGHIERI, *THE DIVINE COMEDY*,
CANTO XIII, VERSES 2-9

1

When Morgana concluded her studies at the nunnery later that Spring at the age of eighteen, Eloise easily convinced her not to move in with Grandmother and Lilian. "It is well for you to continue visiting there and play the part of the doting aunt and affectionate granddaughter, but it would not be a proper place for you to live. You need space to grow your powers. Besides," she added callously, "they do not *really* want you to live in their home anyway."

Morgana, forever insecure, reasoned Eloise was correct, though she abhorred the alternative.

"The proper place for you is at your mother's manor house. You will be able to come and go from there as you please and maintain your standing in society," Eloise croaked. "That will be a great advantage to you in your afterlife. You need not end up a forgotten recluse..."

Like me.

Morgana shuddered at the thought.

Grandmother was disappointed when Morgana declared her intent to move home to her mother's but not surprised. Indeed, she believed it a wise decision. "You will better land a match there than here," she winked.

Her remark, though sincere, cut Morgana to the core and seemed to prove Eloise correct. Grandmother must not have really wanted her, Morgana reasoned, since she did not try to change her mind.

In reality, Grandmother believed marriage was the only sure way to lift her granddaughter's downcast spirit. For though Morgana pretended always to be happy, Grandmother well knew that she carried a deep sadness within her.

In the early weeks of her bitter homecoming, Morgana kept so much to herself that her mother gave up. Igraine was unwilling, on the rare occasions they did speak, to parry the blows Morgana thrust her way. So the two women, mother and daughter, faded and lunged in one winless dual after another.

Meanwhile, Morgana's powers grew considerably. She learned to conjure her own spells instead of merely reciting Eloise's by rote. She learned to use nature's power against itself. She could bend its will and force it to help her even when it disdained her machinations. Her only real limitation was her inability to see into the future. As much as Morgana desired the seeing eye, Eloise would not give it to her. Morgana knew only one other possible teacher—the Vale of Avalon.

Great was the attraction of that enchanted place, ruled as it was by the Lady Nimue and frequented, or so alleged, by none other than the famed sorcerer Merlin. It was said to be a place of awesome powers, a gateway between this world, with all its limitations, and the next, so unfathomably infinite. Somehow, Morgana knew the Vale of Avalon could reveal all things and make everything in her life clear. She needed its power. If only she could find her way out of the shadows.

It was in this sad, secretive manner that Morgana spent eight years preparing for the second part of her quest. As in the first part, she knew little about the nature of the threat beyond its appointed day— Lilian's thirteenth birthday.

"I leave on the morrow for Grandmother's," Morgana told her mother when the time was at hand. A storm gathered in her eyes as she prepared her next blow. *Yes, I would rather be with her than you!*

Though Igraine disliked her mother-in-law and was even jealous of the perceived intimacy she had with her daughter, she replied, "Prithee, send my regards to your grandmother." Highly skilled in the art of emotional fencing, she knew not to engage the feint.

"Yes, Mother," Morgana replied with curled lips. "I will be sure to tell her how well you are faring." Her eyes crackled with irony, full knowing her mother was grieving the loss of yet another husband. *Single and alone as you are!* She relished the discomfort her trips to Grandmother brought upon Mother.

Grandmother and Lilian were, of course, eagerly anticipating Morgana's visit. They washed and scrubbed the cottage with added vigor and prepared rich meals. In fact, Lilian's birthday had become more a celebration of Morgana than the birthday girl herself. In keeping with this, Lilian greeted Morgana with the promise of a song in her honor.

"I learned it lately in town from a Cornish minstrel by the name of Tristam," Lilian recalled in a girlish fashion. "He said his heart plagues him with sorrow, and the only way to ease his pain is to sing about it. Tears seemed to flow from his lute as he sang."

"My, you have grown into a young lady," mused Morgana as she looked Lilian over with raised eyebrows. Her face, which was no longer that of a little girl, was exceedingly beautiful. She wore a touch of womanhood on her slim figure. Even the crucifix that rested gracefully around her neck added to the impression of Lilian's maturing beauty.

Lilian giggled as she replied, "Grandmother says I best grow into a lady sometime soon, or I will end up an old spinster."

"That would indeed be a tragedy," Morgana replied sourly, momentarily slipping into her colder character and thinking about her own diminishing marriage prospects. A woman in her twenties, no matter her claim of privilege, faded faster than the winter sun.

Lilian sang the minstrel's sad tale as promised that evening. Her voice, soft and low, was unlike any Morgana had heard before.

Alas my heart, you do me wrong
To cast me off discourteously;

For I have drunken wine too strong,
Been poisoned with its misery.
Fair Iseault 'twas all my joy;
Fair Iseault 'twas my delight;
Fair Iseault 'twas my heart of gold;
But we 'twas poisoned with the dark of night...

The fire crackled in the background and cast shadows of Lilian's silhouette on the foreboding tapestry of the Garden of Eden. By the dim light, she appeared no longer a young girl but a woman, grown and captivating. Yet, there was in her neither lust nor immodesty, only Truth, pure and innocent.

As she sang, the words seared Morgana's heart, but the emotion it called forth was something she could not name. So removed was she from her innermost feelings that Morgana knew not what stirred within her. Was it empathy for the ill-fated lovers of whom Lilian sang? Was it a longing for love and companionship in her own life? Or was it, perhaps, the looming shadow of fear about the consequences of the path she had chosen? Morgana did not indulge her emotions long enough to find out. When the song ended, she clapped her hands in applause and silenced her heart.

"Beautiful, my love. You sang beautifully!" Morgana cooed. *Almost prophetically.*

"Better than the minstrel himself!" Grandmother beamed. "Now, off to bed with you. We want to get a good start on the morrow so we have ample time in the market. Lord knows I have a fat purse full of chinkers!"

"The market?" Morgana inquired.

"Aye, Lilian is going to pick out material for her first gown," Grandmother replied. "And that means we must wake extra early to complete our chores around the cottage; so off to bed, the both of you."

That must be it—something in the market, or perhaps along the way.

Morgana examined her face in the looking glass by her bedside. She relished the idea of saving Lilian yet again, but her pleasure was born more out of selfishness than concern for her niece. Indeed, Morgana was so confident in her powers that she was none too worried about Lilian's well-being. Instead, her veins pulsated with the desire to win the type of overflowing gratitude that she failed to gain from Grandmother and Lilian after the first quest. She wanted their approval, their acceptance, their love above all else. Little did she know that she had always had it.

"If only I had a spell for *you*," Morgana said, talking to the faint wrinkles forming across her forehead.

The mirror had become her enemy. It reflected a cold, bitter image that taunted Morgana and made her feel old and ugly like Eloise. Disdainfully, she looked away and set her eyes on the crucifix on the wall, the very same one from all those years ago. It now appeared no different than any other adornment in the room. Morgana smiled smugly, thinking herself much wiser than during those eight years hence, and snuffed out her candle.

2

The next morning, Lilian's thirteenth birthday, Morgana awoke well before the first rooster crowed but refused to rise. Such was her custom ever since she had finished her studies at the nunnery. It was a form of protest, a rejection of the rigid schedule she had previously been forced to keep. She lay in bed, pondering the possible threats that could unfold and the many spells she could use in each scenario. It must be something grand, something magnificent, yet not too much so as to arouse suspicions. Just as Eloise had cautioned, Grandmother and Lilian must never know of her powers. If it came down to it, she could always cast a spell to make them unaware of what transpired, but Morgana was reluctant to pursue that course. It was too easy to outright blind them, and what was the fun in that? She wanted the challenge of performing everything in secret before their very eyes. How else could she win their gratitude?

As the sound of Grandmother's early morning shuffling began to get louder and louder, Morgana at last gave in to the pressure to get up. The old lady obviously wanted Morgana to come down and join her. She would feign a disinterest in having help with breakfast, but both knew better, and both would readily fall into their prescribed roles. Grandmother would play the part of the overworked homemaker, and Morgana would do her best to lessen her load but with little effect, of course, for Grandmother would never permit a guest—even Morgana—to do much real work. All she really wanted was company, a chance to visit with her granddaughter.

By and by, the three ladies set out in the carriage with Grandmother at the reigns. The grass was wet with dew, and the sun shone pink and orange overhead as it continued to make its morning ascent. Morgana sat guardedly, listening to Grandmother's idle chatter and watching Lilian swing her feet in a girlish fashion.

She is so young still. If only she were not so eager to grow up.

At the market, Lilian bounced from one stall to another, innocently fingering many fine fabrics, while Grandmother and Morgana perused with distant curiosity, neither suggesting interest in nor dismissing any particular material outright. Such was the more sensible approach to haggling, they explained to Lilian discreetly. Still, the young lady could not contain her excitement and would have carried away every last bolt of fabric if she could have.

"How about this one, Love?" Grandmother finally asked, indicating a tasteful green silk linen.

"It is sophisticated *and* age-appropriate."

Lilian glanced over, reluctant to let go of the crimson red fabric she had fixated on. Too kind to speak her mind, she said meekly, "It is quite nice, Grandmother."

Oh, please!

The girl's graciousness was too much for Morgana, who could not stand the thought of walking away with something that would not be truly pleasing to everyone. She flicked her wrist, and a moment later the merchant pulled out a lavish blue fabric, embroidered with a fine, golden cross-stitch pattern.

"Perchance something like this will suit the young lady," he offered unexpectedly. Though he knew it not, Morgana's powers had compelled him to show off his finest fabric, material he kept in reserve for special, high-paying customers only.

Lilian's eyes grew wide, but she checked her impulse to reach for it. She knew such fabric was far too exquisite to consider, no matter how many chinkers Grandmother had saved up.

"Indeed," Grandmother replied haughtily, too proud to walk away but full knowing her purse could not afford it.

"It just arrived from France," he explained, "and none too soon, it would seem. It matches her budding beauty perfectly." A true salesman, he knew precisely what to say to please Grandmother and Lilian, not that he actually wanted to sell the fabric to such ordinary customers. "Though I am afraid the price is quite exorbitant."

"Humph," was all Grandmother could reply as she began to inch toward the next stall.

Then with another flick of Morgana's wrist, the merchant called them back. "I am not an unreasonable man. Prithee, name a price."

And so began the customary round of dickering, which, through Morgana's powers, worked out much to Grandmother's advantage.

"Will you require a tailor?" the merchant asked at last, hoping to regain some ground.

"Goodness, no!" Grandmother replied with mock offense. "I have dressed many fine ladies in my day. I would have to be cold in the grave before I would let another sew my granddaughter's first gown!"

When the transaction was concluded to Grandmother's satisfaction, the women once again set out in the carriage for their return voyage home. Lilian held the small parcel containing her new fabric with a protectiveness that suggested far greater contents. Her eyes beamed with happiness and gratitude. Likewise, Grandmother quietly congratulated herself on striking such a good bargain. Even Morgana could not help but feel a tinge of warmth from the morning's outing. Though she hated to admit it, Morgana enjoyed shopping for the fabric and envisioning the cut and style of the new gown nearly as much as Lilian herself. How simple Morgana's life could have been if she were free to live as a lady should, free to hope and dream and marry. A sigh formed in her chest, and she exhaled coolly, gliding her hands down the folds of her skirt and recalling Eloise's admonishments of the past.

Self-pity will weaken your ability to accomplish great things. You will feel held back and powerless; you will see yourself as a victim, and there is nothing so pathetic. You must be master of your own fate.

The carriage suddenly jolted up and down and then came to an abrupt stop. Morgana and Lilian lithely dismounted from the carriage and inspected the situation. In a moment's glance, they observed Grandmother had driven over a divet and cracked the right front wheel. There was no way for the trio to fix it, at least without magic, and such a display would be far too obvious

"We best continue to the cottage on foot," reasoned Grandmother. "We can send a worker back to replace the wheel on the morrow. Gather what you can carry."

Fortunately, aside from the fabric and Grandmother's purse, the women had little of value with them. Lilian tied her precious parcel to her back and offered her arm to Grandmother. The latter was still quite robust in her old age, but she was tired from the long outing and upset about her careless driving accident. She pretended to be in good spirits, but Morgana correctly sensed otherwise.

"Shall we sit and rest a bit?" Morgana suggested after they had completed the first mile and Grandmother's exhaustion became apparent.

"I can fetch a driver?" Lilian offered.

Before Grandmother could respond, Morgana

took charge. "It is too late in the day for us to separate. I fear harm may befall us if we do not stick together."

Though she spoke truly, her calculation was more complex than she let on. Not only was Morgana reluctant to let Lilian out of her sight in light of the impending threat on her life, but she also preferred to have the entire party witness her rescue, which she now felt assured was imminent.

"We can cut through the woods and lessen our journey by half. We will have but two more miles ahead of us. I know the route well from having taken it with Father as a child. It could not have changed much," Morgana declared authoritatively.

"Then it is settled," Grandmother replied as if she had determined their course of action herself. She was not used to giving up charge. "Gorlois loved these woods…"

Despite her effort to sound nonchalant, the thought of her son troubled her. Perhaps it was a premonition of things to come.

Morgana surveyed the area and gathered her bearings as they walked into the woods and left the main road and sunshine behind them. The trail looked much as she remembered and appeared to still be in good use. Late afternoon rays peaked through the leaves and cast clusters of brightness against the shadows that danced off the mossy trees. Beautiful as it was, Morgana had little time for romanticizing their predicament. She reasoned they would have two more hours of visibility before darkness totally set in. Even at their slow pace, that should be plenty of time to get back to the cottage —unless Fate had other plans, and, indeed she hoped he did, for Morgana was eager to use her powers. Glancing around, she spotted a long, thick branch that could double as a walking staff and a club.

"Sing us a song, Dear," Grandmother requested of Lilian. She wanted something to take her mind off her worries.

Lilian complied, albeit a little self-consciously, and her somber melody carried through the forest like a breathy whisper.

Alas my heart, you do me wrong
To cast me off discourteously…

Morgana cut her arms across her front and signaled for silence—*danger!* In the distance, she saw dark shapes moving in their direction. "Boars. Stay calm. They will not bother us unless we frighten them."

Her father had said the very same thing several times when they had spotted sounders of boars on their treks. Though she did not need proof of Father's wisdom, she certainly got it one day when they witnessed from afar a horrific boar attack on another traveler who was accompanied by a dog. All would have been fine if the dog had not started yelping at the young boar, likely a curious female, who approached. In the mayhem that ensued, the dog was killed on the spot, and the traveler died of his grievous wounds a few painful days later. Father had shielded her eyes, but the sound of the boar goring the dog and man had stayed with her all these years. She shivered at the memory and momentarily pounded her forehead. A voice—her father's—was trying to resurface.

Morgana...

She would not hear it, not yet anyway. Not until her quest was complete.

"We will wait and see which way they go. If they continue this way, we will let them walk around us," commanded Morgana.

And so they waited for what seemed like an eternity while the boars meandered along the trail, rooting around in no clear direction. Then, in near unison, their snouts rose high in the air, and they began walking with a purpose straight toward the women.

"They have caught our scent," Morgana declared. "Let them sniff, but, no matter what, do not call out or strike out at them."

The sounder was upon them in no time at all. Morgana stepped forward slightly and discreetly grounded her staff before her and uttered an inaudible incantation:

Brilliant beams and brazen blisters,
Send the sounder round us sisters.

If the other women had looked down, they would have seen a faint ripple in the grass radiate out in the direction of the boars and heat the terrain under their hooves. No sooner were they caught in the blistering undulation, then the boars grunted and moved on.

"Thanks be to God!" Grandmother dared to exclaim once the sounder was well past. "The Good

Lord surely heard our prayers today."

Neither Morgana nor Lilian responded, but both sighed—Lilian in relief and Morgana in regret. The latter had hoped for something more dramatic. Surely, she had not been preparing all these years to simply shoo away a handful of boars. She could gain no credit for something so trivial.

3

Though she still felt self-conscience and more than a little bit nervous, Lilian began singing again at Grandmother's request.

For I have drunken wine too strong,
Been poisoned with its misery...

They had but half a mile more to go when Grandmother asked to take another break. "I must rest my legs a bit," she stated wearily, regretful of her weakened state. "I feel like a bag of bones today."

Her breathing was more labored than Morgana would have expected, even for one so old, as Grandmother had always been full enough of energy to match a woman half her age.

"We have little time before dark," Morgana protested. "But..." feeling a tinge of guilt at her lack of compassion, she added reluctantly, "we can spare a few minutes for you to regain your strength."

Lilian proceeded to lead Grandmother to a comfortable spot, which captured what remained of the dimming sunlight, while Morgana kept her eyes on the trail.

Darkness lurks.

The irony of her own presence was lost on Morgana. She watched and waited on high alert, trying not to grow tense. The slightest weakness, be it fear or doubt or fatigue, could disarm her powers. She closed her eyes and took a deep breath. That was when she felt the presence of the wolf pack moving in. Though still out of sight, she knew the wolves were attempting to surround them and cut off their chance of escape. It was too late to flee safely; they must fight.

Morgana let out a long, cleansing breath, raised her staff, and allowed its weight to spin her in the direction of Grandmother and Lilian, neither of whom were even remotely aware of the predators. With a sweep of her staff, Morgana sealed them into an invisible dome. Then, she stepped softly toward them and said half-truthfully, "The boars must have stirred up the wildlife. I heard a rustling in the woods just now. Prithee, sit quietly while I investigate."

"Be careful, Morgana," Grandmother uttered wearily. She had little energy and could only pray her granddaughter was mistaken.

"Of course," Morgana replied gruffly, but just as she was turning away, something compelled her to look back. Weak and fragile as Grandmother appeared, she had an unexpected beauty about her. It was the look of one who is full of grace, one at peace. How Grandmother had suffered throughout her life! But none would know it to look at her. She bore all with dignity. Morgana felt ashamed for not being a better granddaughter, and she realized no one else in the world loved her like she did—not Eloise and certainly not her own mother. Touched with unexpected compassion, Morgana inclined her head, smiled reassuringly, and then turned back to the work at hand.

The wolves were still in hiding, but Morgana was able to easily determine their locations. There were three in all—two guarding the path and one circling around to cut them off from behind. She sensed they were nearly in position. The pair on the path would attack first, and the one in the rear would wait to move in until escape was completely cut off. Morgana felt a rush of excitement when the two pale shadows emerged side by side. Their growls started out as a low rumble and grew louder as their lips curled back and revealed ravenous fangs. From the look of their gaunt frames, the wolves had not eaten in days and were starved for flesh. Slowly, they crept forward. Their posture seemed to dare Morgana to act.

Why not? Morgana cackled to herself as if in reply. She could barely contain her excitement as she continued silently:

> *Shadows sharpen, boulders buckle,*
> *Make my staff a lethal knuckle.*
> *Guide my hands and set my feet,*
> *To knock and blast all foes I meet.*

Morgana stepped forward and held up her staff just as the first wolf pounced. With unexpected force, she clobbered the wolf over the head and knocked it senseless. She brought the staff back up just in time to swing at the second wolf. Stronger than his partner, he caught the staff in his teeth and writhed furiously, sending frothy slobber flying in the air. The wolf's blood-curdling growl drowned out the cries from Lilian and Grandmother. The only thing Morgana could focus on was killing the wolf and killing it quickly. She knew the final wolf would emerge at any moment, and she did not want to make her powers too obvious. She locked eyes with the wolf and began twisting the staff and thrusting it deeper into its throat. Then, she uttered something garbled and rammed the staff all the way down its throat, spilling a pool of blood out of its lifeless mouth.

There was no time to celebrate. Morgana turned in a fury and moved with haste toward Grandmother and Lilian. When she was but a few feet from the women, she saw the final wolf brazenly step forward. He was nearly twice the size of the other two though just as gaunt.

He must be the head of the pack.

But before she could raise her staff, an arrow whizzed through the air and pierced the wolf in its throat. Lilian swooned into a faint, and a young man with golden locks about his shoulders stepped out into the clearing.

Aghast, Morgana looked him up and down. He was perhaps five to ten years younger than Morgana, but she could not be certain. Broad shouldered yet graceful in his build, he was quite fair to behold. He wore the dress of a woodsman, though his garments were exquisitely made. His tunic, which was tied with a simple leather belt, was uncommonly white and bore golden embellishments about the edges. His cloak was a creamy brown and hung over one shoulder only, revealing an arrow quiver on his back that was matched by the finely crafted bow in his hand. Even his leggings, hose, and boots had a refined quality to them.

Mistaking Morgana's hostility for terror, the young man knelt, bowed his head, and stated, "I fear I have alarmed you when my intention was quite the opposite. I prithee, allow me to be of service. Your party appears to be in distress."

He motioned toward Grandmother and Lilian.

Turning, Morgana could not believe her eyes. Grandmother looked deadly pale and was feebly attempting to awaken Lilian from her faint. The girl was fine, just a little shook up, but Grandmother was in a grave state.

"Grandmother!" Morgana cried out as she disentangled the young girl from the old woman's arms and deposited her into the care of the mysterious stranger. "We are safe now."

"Indeed, we are," Grandmother replied weakly, holding her chest. Her heart was failing from all the strain and distress of their misadventure. "Grammarcy, Morgana…You have been a good girl to me."

Morgana had been so focused on using her powers to protect Lilian that she had not seen the obvious danger to Grandmother. Was this part of her quest? Never mind that. She knew Grandmother's death was something she could not have prepared for even if she had tried. Morgana held Grandmother's hand but could not find the words to speak. There was no need. True to form, Grandmother would not waste her final breaths listening. She was determined to have Morgana hear her out once and for all.

"My beauteous granddaughter," she began. "Most beloved child of my only son, how I have prayed for you through the years. You must allow the light of God to overcome the shadows that have grown in your heart. Time and again I tried to dismiss my fears for you as the fanciful imaginations of an old lady, but—*truly*—I have known all along that *she* got a hold of you." Grandmother flinched as her heart tightened beneath her chest. "You can break free if you ask for the God's help. Lord knows he gave it to me."

Morgana was overcome by a torrent of emotions. She felt helpless, confused, shameful, but, most of all, she felt remorse—for her rejection of Grandmother's love, for not having been more aware of Grandmother's failing health, and for being unable to prevent her death.

Another death.

"I should have let you leave the convent and care for Lilian alongside me all those years ago," Grandmother continued. "Prithee, forgive me, Morgana, and do me the honor of caring for Lilian in my stead now. She needs you."

"I would not know how…" Morgana replied honestly.

"No one really *knows* how to raise another, but people do it all the time. Trust your heart and pray," Grandmother replied as she feebly placed her Rosary beads in Morgana's hands. Her voice was fainter now. "Send her to me."

Morgana looked on unable to hear Grandmother's final words to Lilian. The young girl remained composed. Her shoulders sagged only slightly while her head nodded in assent. Then, she reached forward and gathered Grandmother close into her chest and began singing a hymn.

Be near when I am dying,
O show Thou cross to me!
And, for my succor flying,
Come, Lord, to set me free.

Her voice carried through the dusky woods and seemed to take Grandmother's soul along with it up to Heaven.

These eyes new faith receiving,
From Thee shall never move;
For he who dies believing,
Dies safely in Thy love.

It was a song to make the coldest melt. Morgana, senseless to everything, looked blindly as the handsome young woodsman stepped forward and lifted Grandmother in his arms.

"Let us depart. Wild animals will not take pity on you for your loss."

Unable to refuse, the women accepted his

escort back to the cottage. They walked swiftly but with a heaviness about their persons and said nothing until they got back home.

"If you will permit, I will gladly return on the morrow with religious to bury your grandmother," the woodsman said.

"And to whom should we express our gratitude?" asked Morgana bitterly, holding back tears. She resented his intrusion.

"I am called Lancelot of the Lake," he replied with a slight bow of his head, "and I hope you will not refuse my help, stranger though I may be."

If Morgana had not been so distraught, she would have turned him down. "Very well," she replied reluctantly, bowing in turn. Acceptance seemed the surest way to conclude the encounter —at least for the time being. Morgana needed space. She needed to think. She needed to rest.

"I must bid you good night," Lancelot said. "My lady is waiting."

"Your lady?" Morgana inquired. Her curiosity urged on her tired mind.

Lilian, who had been quietly listening all the while, inclined her head in eager expectation. She, too, wanted to know the answer.

"Yes, the Lady Nimue," he replied. "She has been a mother to me since before I can remember."

"Until the morrow, then," Morgana answered with sudden intrigue. Nimue, she well knew, was ruler of the Vale of Avalon. Certainly, this twist of Fate could not be a coincidence.

4

Morgana passed a dreadful night sleep in the cottage. Her head, astir with questions, taunted her aching heart. Should she take Lilian as a ward? And what of Grandmother's other wish— for her to embrace God? Having gone so far down the path of darkness, would she be able to turn back even if she wanted to? Would that mean relinquishing her powers? That was something she certainly was not willing to do, not when she had yet to gain retribution on the House of Pendragon and still had not the faintest idea how it would come to pass!

Set as Morgana was on the black arts, she could not easily dismiss Grandmother's dying wishes altogether. And so it was decided. She would send word to Mother of Grandmother's death and declare her intent to take over the property, which was hers by right. Mother would disapprove, of course, but that was no matter. Igraine had long since lost her authority.

Eloise would not be pleased either, but blast it all! Morgana had had enough of Eloise telling her what to do. She was not a novice anymore, and perhaps she *should* break free from her tutelage as Grandmother had urged. The old lady obviously knew more than what she had ever let on, but how? Morgana tossed the matter over all night long but could find no reason why living with Lilian in the cottage would hurt her quest. If anything, it would make it easier, she reasoned. Whatever role Morgana's heart played in her decision that day, she ignored it. Instead, she told herself that her decision was based purely on sound judgment.

Lilian was already busy in the cottage when Morgana finally stirred from her room the next morning. A hearty breakfast of bread, cheese, and poached eggs was set on the table, and the main room looked immaculate. Lilian was determined to carry on fastidiously. Though her sorrow showed, it could not dim her budding beauty. Indeed, Morgana thought she looked more womanly than ever dressed in black mourning.

"Good morrow, Aunt," Lilian smiled meekly. "I hope my preparations did not disturb you."

"Certainly not, Lilian," Morgana replied pulling out a chair. "Prithee, sit a moment so we can talk."

Lilian obediently complied, and Morgana began, "I know the events of yesterday have been hard on you—on all of us—but you need not fear for your own well-being. I will care for you in Grandmother's stead."

Lilian's eyes brightened as she replied, "I am glad of it, though I fear you sacrifice too much. Prithee, do not feel obligated…"

"I will hear no such talk," Morgana interrupted. "I have freely chosen to stay and look after you. This was my home once, too, and it was a happy one. It will be so again in time."

Morgana almost believed herself as she spoke the words. Her midnight resolution was now set in motion, and she felt in command. In a voice that sounded much like Grandmother's, she continued, "We must eat now, Love, before the burial party arrives."

Morgana placed a napkin on her lap and reached for the bread when she heard Lilian invoke the Sign of the Cross. What a careless mistake! Her hand recoiled one into the other, and she bowed her head. Though the words rang out of her mouth with piety, Morgana pushed them as far from her heart as possible.

"Bless us, O Lord…"

Barely had they finished eating when the somber chanting of the burial procession could be heard. Lancelot led a party of three monks dressed in dark hooded habits. Morgana's heart started to beat more rapidly. Was she merely excited about the new twist in her quest? At that time, perhaps.

The burial took but a few hours. It was a somber event made lighter only by the velvety sound of Lilian's voice harmonizing with the melancholy chanting of the monks. Morgana knew the Latin prayers by rote and chanted them as if in a trance. Her voice in song was neither beautiful nor ugly. It simply blended in, emotionless and unimaginative. The only hint of feeling one could have discerned from her was when the first shovel of dirt was thrown on Grandmother's shrouded body. Morgana winced. She felt not only the pain of Grandmother's death but that of her father's and Roselyn's all over again. Irrational as it was, she blamed Uther for all of it.

When the ceremony was over, she assumed her newly acquired role as head of the house and expressed her gratitude to the burial party. The monks offered a few modest bereavement gifts to help the women in their new situation—a sack of flour and a jar of cooking oil. Though Morgana was used to splendor at her mother's manor house, she knew these gifts were of the more practical kind that her new lifestyle required.

"I am relieved to hear Lancelot will be checking in on you," said one of the elderly monks. "He is a fine young man whom you can look to for assistance."

"Lancelot checking in on us? Of this I was not aware," Morgana replied, cutting a glance at Lancelot. He stood a few yards off and was listening in on the conversation. "But I would be most pleased to have his protective eye about our cottage," she added.

Lilian smiled in agreement, and the party said their farewells. Only Lancelot lingered a moment. He approached Lilian, looked into her teary eyes, and said, "My deepest condolences on your loss. I know what it is to lose someone you love. This too shall pass."

"So Grandmother told me," she replied, "but

she did not say *how* I am to overcome the pain in the meantime."

"Trust in God," assured Lancelot. His blue eyes brimmed with sincerity. "I hope to find you in happier spirits when next I call on you and Lady Morgana."

"I hope so, too," she returned. The thought of him calling already softened the pain

5

Lilian and Morgana passed the rest of the day quietly working about the house. There was little that needed to be done, but both felt the urge to fill the void of Grandmother's death with distractions. When there was nothing left to polish and re-polish, Lilian stood before Grandmother's loom and examined the half-finished tapestry stretched across it.

"It will be a shame to lose Lord Ryon's commission," Lilian mused aloud.

"It is no matter. I have financial means to support us," replied Morgana without looking up. She was writing to Mother. "I shall write him next with news of Grandmother's death."

"I could complete it—the tapestry, that is," replied Lilian tepidly. "Grandmother often had me sit and work the strings for her."

Really? Morgana knew Lilian was gifted but the idea she had acquired enough skill to complete such an enormous, let alone prestigious, task was absurd. "Lilian, I fear this is beyond your powers—at least at this time. Perchance with more training…"

"Is there harm in trying?" Lilian rejoined with unexpected boldness.

I never! Morgana softened her voice to mask her irritation and said, "Love, you could not possibly replicate Grandmother's skill, and that is saying nothing about her pattern. You know as well as I that she never wrote them down."

"I do not mean to suggest I am nor could ever be as skilled as Grandmother was, but..." Lilian paused, "she had me design this one as part of my schooling. I can show you the pattern if you would like."

Morgana looked over the tapestry, matching it up with the carefully drawn pattern Lilian presented. The color scheme was just as magnificent as any other tapestry Grandmother had completed, only it had a gentleness about it that was uncharacteristic of her usual, more vibrant designs.

"What is it to depict?" Morgana asked with keen interest as her eyes surveyed the figures.

"It tells the story of the white hart, the brachet, and the damsel," she began, pointing out each in turn. "One day, the hart, with the brachet nipping at its legs, ran into the hall of a great king. Then, a knight rose up and stole off with the brachet and scared away the hart. No sooner did that occur then a fair damsel entered and claimed the brachet as her own and implored succor from the king who kindly sent his three best knights in pursuit..."

Lilian grew more animated as she revealed intricate details far beyond the scene itself, which, she explained, would set the stage for a great quest. Two of the king's knights would fail to achieve it, but one would succeed because of his selfless humility.

"What a captivating imagination you have!" Morgana said with a smile when the tale was through. "How did you ever think of such a story?"

"It was merely a dream I dreamt, a childish fantasy. Grandmother loved to hear me ramble on about it," Lilian reminisced.

Morgana turned her curious eye from the canvas to Lilian. "I could almost believe it had all happened…"

"If only we lived in a world where it could," Lilian sighed. "Prithee, Aunt Morgana, permit me to finish the tapestry? If Lord Ryon no longer desires it by my hand, surely it would still be worthy of a lesser house."

"Quite true. Very well," Morgana consented. It would give the girl some amusement and afford Morgana some space. It actually was a promising work. In the right hands it would be exquisite.

In between slyly practicing her magic, Morgana would mark the progress Lilian made on the tapestry. It was evident Lilian had not only been a good student of the craft, absorbing everything from Grandmother's technique to her sitting posture, but that she also possessed an inborn gift for weaving. With more practice, she would eventually surpass Grandmother for she possessed a finer hand and more discerning eye for beauty.

And so the time passed with little excitement

save periodic visits from Lancelot. It is no wonder Lilian was smitten. He was as kind and good-natured, handsome and charming, as she was young and hopeful, beautiful and alluring. Morgana's fondness, however, was more difficult to account for, aged and hardened as she was. The trio would walk the countryside and make idle chatter about the events of the kingdom. On one such outing, Morgana at last dared to inquire about the Lady Nimue.

"Are the stories of her powers true?" she asked.

"I know not of what stories you speak." His laugh suggested otherwise. "But right verily she possesses great powers. Much has she accomplished through her goodness, not only for me, but for the Realm of Logres. Of this, however, I cannot speak."

"It must have been hard growing up without a mother," Lilian interjected. The words slipped out without thinking. She did not want to pry or seem to pity Lancelot. Indeed, she had never given into self-pity over the absence of her own mother nor, more recently, of Grandmother.

"You speak truly, but I have been graced with the maternal care of one whose love is as selfless as that of a mother," Lancelot replied. "Love from another is what matters in the end. It is always within reach—if you simply look for it."

His words, full of meaning, were personalized by each lady. Lilian felt a kinship with Lancelot as she recalled Grandmother's warm care and gave thanks for Morgana's guardianship. She suddenly felt certain Lancelot understood her better than anyone else in the world and hoped she might someday be his lady. Likewise, Morgana thought his words were meant just for her. She took them as a tender commendation for her willingness to care for Lilian, an expression of admiration if not burgeoning love.

If only he would speak plainly…

"Can you tell me of my mother?" Lilian asked Morgana later that evening as she wove a colorful spray of silken thread across the warp strings of the loom. "Grandmother said she was a dear friend of yours."

Morgana put down her writing and turned to Lilian. "What else did she tell you?"

Lilian looked down at the thread in her hands, too uncomfortable to face Morgana directly. "Only that my mother died giving birth to me and that you brought me hither."

"There is little else to tell, Lilian," Morgana replied as memories of her departed friend forced their way to the surface.

"Prithee, Aunt, tell me what she was like!" Lilian implored softly. "What did she look like? What made her laugh? What did she love?"

"She loved *you*, Lilian. She would talk for hours about the life she wanted for you. She wondered if you would have her golden hair and blue eyes or the darker coloring of your father. She wanted to share her love of nature with you," Morgana replied as one in a daydream. "She imagined taking you to pick wild flowers and climb trees. Mostly, she would talk about how she would teach you to be strong, to withstand heartache and scrutiny. That was why I knew Grandmother would be the right person to raise you in her stead…"

It felt good to talk of her old friend. It reminded Morgana of a more promising time in her life, a time when she was happy in a way, free, though she had not realized it then. Morgana spoke openly, omitting anything to do with Eloise, of course, but sharing more than she would have thought capable of remembering.

"And what of my father?" Lilian asked.

"I inquired about him after your mother died but found no trace of him," Morgana responded. "I fear he is gone, too, one way or the other."

"Grammarcy, Aunt Morgana," Lilian said after a long pause.

"For what? I have little to offer besides memories of a time long past," Morgana replied.

"I will cherish those memories as if they were my own. And I thank you most heartily for finding me a home then and preserving it for me now," Lilian replied. "You are all I have left of my family."

Morgana, overcome with emotion, placed her hand on her heart. She felt an urge to protect Lilian as she had originally planned those many years ago when she brought the orphaned babe to Grandmother's—not, as it had become, for the sake of revenge or self-aggrandizing—but for love, real, true love.

"Your mother would be proud of you," was all Morgana could manage without crying. "I hope to make her proud of me, too."

Part IV

To the Tower

We turned our backs upon that dismal valley
by climbing up the bank that girdles it;
we made our way across without a word.
Here it was less than night and less than day,
so that my sight could only move ahead
slightly, but then I heard a bugle blast
so strong, it would have made a thunder clap
seem faint; at this, my eyes—which doubled
back upon their path—turned fully toward one
place.

- DANTE ALIGHIERI, *THE DIVINE COMEDY*,
CANTO XXXI, VERSES 7-15

1

Once true love flowed from Morgana's heart, she could not stop herself from feeling all sorts of other emotions, the most dominant of which was remorse. Day after day, she walked the countryside and contemplated her life. She desired to change, to be good again—if she ever was—but knew not how. It was not that she was lacking in will, for Morgana's was strong, but that she worried what would become of Lilian if she gave up the black arts. Sorcery seemed the only full-proof option of saving her from the final threat on her life. And what of Morgana's thirst for revenge on the House of Pendragon? Sometimes it would flicker and flare up ravenously; at others, it would die down almost enough for her to overcome it. Did she attempt forgiveness? Certainly not! But, she at least tried to put her thirst for revenge behind her.

For her part, Lilian tended the house and developed her hand at the loom. She missed Grandmother terribly, but, by the time Lord Ryon's tapestry was complete, Lilian's pain had subsided, and her bond with Morgana had turned a new page in her life.

Lilian began confiding her girlish hopes for love, marriage, and children, and soon came to reveal her feelings for Lancelot. Morgana was not the least surprised, of course. Lilian's affections were plain to see. What she was surprised about was her own reaction to the news. Though she longed for Lancelot's attention as well, she managed to squelch her jealousy. With Lilian being three years younger than Lancelot and Morgana a full decade older, the former was obviously the better match for him— and that was saying nothing of their characters. Still, Morgana secretly hoped she might be worthy of Lancelot's affections if not someone else like him. She took his every word and smile as a promise of a better life.

"Aunt, you just missed Lancelot," Lilian began one warm summer evening when Morgana returned from a walk. "He asked me to send his greetings."

"That was kind of him," Morgana replied, trying not to show her disappointment at not seeing him. "Did he stay long?"

"A couple hours only. I asked him to join us for supper, but he said he could not," Lilian sighed.

"Tell me, what did you speak of during all that time?" asked Morgana as she fanned herself by the window. The air was warm and dry, almost suffocating.

"I told him of the new tapestry Lord Ryon commissioned," Lilian answered smiling. "And he said my imagination is running away again."

"I dare say he is right. To think, a knight green all over and with a green horse to match!" Morgana replied teasingly. "Come, now. What else did you speak of?"

"What else does he ever speak of but knighthood?" Lilian replied dreamily. "As always, he seeks a lord to whom he can pledge his fealty. I wish he would seek a lady first."

"So do I," sighed Morgana thinking of herself. *To be Lancelot's lady!*

"He would make a fine knight, would he not, Aunt Morgana?" Lilian continued.

"He would indeed, Love, but you should not encourage him too much," Morgana responded.

Lilian was confused. "I do not understand your meaning."

"I fear knighthood would take him from us," Morgana replied delicately, "and then who would we have to check in on us and keep us company?"

"Surely, he would not leave us unattended," Lilian protested.

"Indeed not. Lancelot is far too concerned with our well-being to do such a thing, but," Morgana teased, "the monks would be a poor substitute, no matter how comely they may look in their brown robes."

Lilian blushed, and Morgana laughed at her embarrassment.

"Perhaps knighthood would steal him away, but…" Lilian began. Her mind was far off. She imagined Lancelot pledging his love for her and dedicating his quests in her honor. "But he would be back. I do not doubt his intentions."

"Nor do I," Morgana said in return. "But Fate has little regard for our wishes."

At times like those, Morgana wished desperately to be free of her quest, to be without responsibility for the happiness of another. Her mind would turn to the one person who seemed to have a command of everything—Eloise. The two had not spoken since Morgana had taken up permanent residence at the cottage. It was not that Morgana deliberately avoided meeting Eloise, but that she kept putting it off. She knew a meeting would force her to choose between the new life she hoped for and the dark path she felt driven down.

So when she heard a gentle rap on the door the day before Lilian's fifteenth birthday, Morgana's heart sank.

"I have been expecting you, Eloise," Morgana began. "Prithee, enter."

"Grammarcy, Morgana dear. A cynical woman would not have expected a warm welcome after two years of silence," Eloise offered with a wry smile on her face. Time seemed to have changed her only slightly. Her wrinkles were a little deeper, her frame a little frailer, but her eyes appeared sharper than ever. "I trust the girl is out?"

"Yes, we may talk freely. Lilian has gone to town and will not be back for at least another hour," Morgana replied. Her heart pounded inside her chest, just as it had at their first meeting so long ago. She felt again the pupil, ignorant and afraid. Yet, Morgana knew she needed to be strong and masterful, to match wit for wit. If she had learned anything during her daily reflections in the countryside, it was that Eloise's influence could be manipulative.

"You know, of course, what brings me. The final part of your quest will take place a year and a day hence. We must begin making preparations now," Eloise said.

"Why so soon?" Morgana asked.

Her question irritated Eloise. "I had hoped the passing of time would grant you greater clarity, but instead, this cottage has blinded you to the obvious. I hope you have not let your powers fade, too!"

"I most certainly have not!" Morgana replied defensively, though she wondered the toll her lack of practice may have taken. "Prithee, speak plainly. What are you trying to tell me?"

After a pointedly agonizing pause, Eloise cleared her crackly throat and said, "You not only let a wolf get away on her thirteenth birthday, but he has been living in your midst these years hence."

Morgana wanted to protest, but she resisted. "Go on," she said coolly.

"Lancelot of the Lake is not the true and virtuous man he pretends to be. He has a dark secret, so dark in fact he does not yet know it himself." Eloise paused again to let the words take effect. She took pleasure in the act of destroying another's character. "His head will be turned in the court of King Arthur, and he will succumb to the sin of adultery. So great will his stain be, that he will ruin not only himself but the Realm of Logres as well."

Morgana furrowed her brows and narrowed her eyes. "*King Arthur*? Such a king does not exist…not unless…"

"Are you beginning to see now?" Eloise pointed her jagged finger toward a needlework design of a sword in a stone, which Lilian had completed before Grandmother's death. "Yes, your half-brother, Arthur, has come out of hiding at last and proven himself the true-born king of England. Your revenge on the House of Pendragon is finally at hand—if you save Lilian from Lancelot. *He* is the third and final threat."

Lancelot? Impossible. Morgana smoothed the folds of her skirt and weighed all she had been told.

"Your silence conveys doubt. I am sorry for it, for Lilian's sake as much as your own," Eloise said, again clearing her throat.

Morgana would not allow herself to be baited. "Precisely what threat does Lancelot pose to Lilian?"

"His infidelity brings more than heartbreak. It brings death itself!" Eloise declared.

"But how?" Morgana questioned incredulously. "You cannot mean to say that Lancelot would kill Lilian? That he would knowingly hurt her in any way is inconceivable."

"You are taken with him yourself, I see," Eloise mused when she saw Morgana's cheeks momentarily fire with red. "Surely *you* do not hope for marriage at this point in your life. Besides, Lancelot is just a man like any other—vain and impulsive. He cares not for others but that they care for him. Whatever gracefulness and charity you believe to have seen in him is merely a ploy for attention, for aggrandizement. Do not be fooled. Ask yourself," she continued mockingly, "if he has not knowingly led you on while courting Lilian all the while? Come now, be honest with yourself."

Absurd!

It was an impossible notion—Lancelot having a dark side like herself. He was much too good to even think about leading her and Lilian on at the same time, let alone to have an affair and kill one who loves him. His intentions had always been upright, or had they? Morgana's eyes burned as she recalled his many compliments over the last two years. She refused to think Lancelot had been insincere; yet, she knew his heart belonged to Lilian, and she should not have cherished his words so much. If anyone had done wrong, it was she for secretly pining after her niece's suitor.

"How does any of this have to do with the House of Pendragon?" she asked, trying to regain her composure and get back on point.

"That is the best part! Lancelot will commit adultery with Arthur's own wife, and war will ensue, ending the House of Pendragon once and for all," Eloise cackled. "You will have your revenge, and Lilian will have her future. Then…if you desire, you can live a life unburdened."

"And all I would need do is separate Lilian and Lancelot?" Morgana needed to know everything she could.

"In a manner of speaking," Eloise responded.

"Could I not separate Lancelot from Arthur's wife so he stays true to Lilian?" Morgana asked.

"Would you really be willing to forego revenge on the House of Pendragon? Uther slew your father, married your mother, and cast you away when his son was born! He who inherited the crown inherited the guilt!" Eloise raged herself into a phlegmy coughing fit. Between each labored breath she continued, "Even if you were willing to give up your revenge, to let your father's murderer go unpunished, you cannot prevent Lancelot's infidelity. If it be not with Arthur's wife, it will be with another. Lilian will die through his vice all the same. You must separate her from Lancelot before it is too late to prevent her undoing."

Morgana opened her mouth to ask for instructions but stopped short. Her eye caught a sudden movement behind Eloise. It was Grandmother's tapestry of the Garden of Eden, gently aflutter in the windless room. *A sign!* But what could it mean? What was it telling her? Grandmother's dying words floated silently through the silken ripples. *Break free from her!*

"Your counsel has always been sound, but I must take my own this time," Morgana told a surprised Eloise. "I will consider all you have foretold and make my decision in a fortnight."

"Very well," Eloise replied indignantly. "Beware you take no longer, or more sorrow will befall you. Until anon."

Morgana inclined her head, and with a flip of

her hand, the little cottage door swung open, bidding Eloise a cold farewell.

2

After Eloise departed, Morgana once again studied the tapestry of the Garden of Eden. It was magnificent. No matter how many times she gazed at it over the years, she would notice something new—an apple dressed in red and gold or a blossom blushing with purple and pink. Grandmother had always said it was her best work. She had begun it as a commission but could not part with it once it was done. Lord Ryon the Elder was none too happy, but Grandmother settled the affair to his liking in the end. Grandmother used to say she suffered the biggest financial loss of her life over that tapestry, but she would have suffered more had it been needed. She loved the tapestry but not out of vanity. She said it captured the essence of her spiritual pilgrimage. Whenever she felt without direction, she would sit before the tapestry and pray.

Perhaps…

Morgana suddenly rose in pursuit of Grandmother's Rosary beads, which had remained untouched in her room since Grandmother's death. The urge to lean on something, even a prayer she had long scoffed at as empty and meaningless, over-came her. She wanted to unload all her troubles once and for all.

The moment she ascended the first step, however, the front door flew open, and Lilian bounded through in a flurry of excitement.

"You will never believe what news I bring!" Lilian exclaimed. "A modest squire has unwittingly proven himself the true-born king of England! By some strange enchantment, a mysterious sword in a stone appeared before the gates of Camelot. It was said that he who could draw the sword would prove himself king!" Pausing only to take a breath, she continued, "A squire named Arthur did so just yesterday at the great tournament! They say he pulled it out at a touch."

Morgana glanced at Lilian's needlework of the sword and stone, the same one Eloise had observed. "Could she have the gift of the seeing eye?" Morgana wondered. "But how?"

"The king is the very same Arthur who disappeared as a small boy. He is the son of Uther Pendragon, and, I believe…your half-brother."

Morgana had never discussed her personal history with Lilian, and she felt somewhat annoyed at the revelation that Lilian was aware of it. Grand-mother must have shared it with her.

"Indeed," was all Morgana could say. So over-come, she could not even feign a smile.

"Your family has been restored," Lilian pressed with more enthusiasm. She could not understand why Morgana showed so little emotion.

"My family will never be restored," Morgana replied sharply. She could not keep from showing her bitterness. Was it at Arthur, his father, their mother, or all three? Or was it, perhaps, at Eloise for placing an impossible decision before her? In any case, it most certainly was not at Lilian, though the young lady bore the brunt of it.

"I prithee, Aunt, forgive me. I have spoken out of turn. I only hoped to bring you glad tidings, not trouble you with painful memories of the past."

"Oh, Lilian, there is nothing to apologize for," Morgana replied sorrowfully. She felt badly about snapping. "You caught me out of sorts. That is all. I was about to fetch my cloak for a walk when you returned," she lied. "The fresh air always refreshes my spirits. I will be back before sunset. Let us talk more when I return."

Morgana proceeded up the stairs, grabbed her cloak, and opened her nightstand. She shuffled through its contents until she found what she was looking for. After a moment's pause, she clasped Grandmother's Rosary beads and shoved them into her pocket.

The breeze felt cool on Morgana's warm face. She inhaled deeply, hoping the air would reinvigorate her distressed soul. She wove her fingers about the Rosary and rolled her thumb and forefinger around one of the beads, never daring to touch the gold crucifix that hung from its end.

Once or twice she tried to pray, but it was no

use. No sooner did the words form on her lips then they disintegrated into a jumble of distracted thoughts. Morgana felt an answer to her dilemma was within reach if she could only stretch her mind a little farther and grasp it. How foolishly she relied on her own powers.

Her mind remained clouded with questions about the budding relationship between Lilian and Lancelot. They seemed to be a perfect pair, destined for true love and all its trappings. The very prospect of their happiness, however, had always made her sad. After talking to Eloise, she was forced to admit her sadness was, at least in part, born of jealousy. She tried to put her feelings aside and consider the matter reasonably, but it was no use. The cottage had taken such a firm hold of her conscience, she could not make the cold calculations that had once been so easy for her. The best she could do was remind herself that Eloise had always been right in the past. She would need to distance herself from Lancelot and, unfortunately, even from Lilian to make a good decision on their behalf.

"Good afternoon, Lady Morgana!" a familiar voice called.

Morgana shoved the Rosary back into her pocket, turned, and saw none other than Lancelot emerge from the woods. He bowed low before her and went on, "It is a beauteous day for a walk. Is it not? I hope I find you well."

"Indeed," Morgana replied evenly.

"Are you heading in or out?" he asked with an

extra bounce in his step. "I was on my way to share news with you and Lady Lilian."

"I was on my way out, but…" Morgana stopped short. Her first test was before her. Could she turn down an opportunity to be with him?

"Certainly, I do not mean to divert your plans. Perhaps I could serve as your escort and return you back to the cottage when you are ready," he offered.

To refuse his company would be too out of character. "I intend only to gather flowers by the riverside," she said, neither accepting nor rejecting his offer.

Lancelot joined in step with her pace. So full of excitement, he did not immediately recognize Morgana's downcast spirit.

"I wish I may be of better service to you, Lady Morgana," he offered after several minutes of listening to naught but the birds chatter above. "I do hope you will call upon me if you need anything, even just someone to talk to."

Morgana longed to tell him everything. She felt like he would know what to do, like he could dismiss all of Eloise's accusations with a single stroke of his mighty sword. But how could she trust him, or anyone for that matter, when she could not trust her own heart? She reached into her pocket and grasped Grandmother's Rosary in hope of extracting its power. Nothing. It felt cold and lifeless to her touch. Morgana cringed at her foolishness and then plastered a smile to her face and began conversing.

"I suppose you bring news of the new king,"

Morgana began casually. "Lilian learned of his coming earlier today."

"Indeed, I do bear news of the king, but that is not all…" Lancelot replied sheepishly.

"Pray, what else could be more newsworthy?" Morgana inquired.

"I do not know if the kingdom would find it newsworthy, but," he began. "I pray you and Lady Lilian might."

Morgana's instincts hummed with possibilities. It seemed he spoke of something personal. Could it be love?

"Prithee, do not keep your silence," Morgana implored, trying not to sound too eager for an answer. She was as curious as she was concerned about what he may share.

"Long have I mentioned my desire to pledge fealty in knighthood to a worthy lord. After seeking the counsel of the Lady Nimue, I believe the new king is that lord," Lancelot replied.

It was crushing news. Morgana had always known her days in Lancelot's company were numbered, but that was the least of her worries. She feared Eloise's prophecy was beginning to unfold.

"Will you leave the life you have known behind in its entirety?" Morgana questioned, though she felt certain of the answer already.

"I pray not entirely," he replied, pausing as he chose his words. "With your permission, I hope to bring Lady Lilian with me as my bride."

It was just as she feared. "Permission is not mine

to give," Morgana hedged. "Lilian must decide for herself if she wants you as her husband, her lord, her master."

Lancelot was not altogether taken aback by Morgana's response. He knew she abhorred many social conventions, but her coolness suggested doubt about the match, about him. "Then, I beg you for your blessing."

Lancelot was desperate for her assurance. Had Eloise not have corrupted Morgana's mind, he would have received both her permission and blessing with a joyful heart. As it was, Morgana could only fall back into her old deceptions. "Most gladly do I bless your proposal. The rest is up to Lilian," she replied coyly. "When shall you ask her hand?"

"This evening, if it pleases you."

Morgana needed more time than that. "My! You do bring news indeed, though I fear your eagerness lacks in romance. Had you not better plan the affair to *her* liking and hence *your* advantage?"

"I suppose I have been more headstrong than gallant in my designs," he acknowledged. "But I do not know how I could bear to wait any longer. Besides, what more is needed than a heart full of love?"

"Perhaps you are right, but young ladies such as Lilian have a head full of ideas to match *their* full hearts. You had better come up with some ideas of your own!" Morgana was in her element. "Give yourself a fortnight to prepare, no more."

"Fourteen days is like an eternity!" Lancelot protested.

"Not when you are preparing for eternity," Morgana quipped with a smile.

For the rest of their outing, Morgana occasionally placed her hand in her pocket and rolled her fingers around the beads just as she had once been accustomed to do with the talisman. She took comfort in its feel, even though she failed to invoke its power. She simply could not bring herself to pray.

"Lancelot, I must tell you all about the new king!" Lilian burst out as soon as he and Morgana entered the cottage. Her eyes beckoned with excitement as if she knew her own fate was somehow tied to that of King Arthur.

3

When Morgana awoke the following morning, she found Lilian already working about the cottage. The young lady moved from one chore to another dancing to the happy tune of her own singing. So lost was she in thought that she did not notice Morgana at first.

"Oh, there you are, Aunt!" she expressed in surprise.

"Good morrow, Lilian," Morgana said wearily. She was unsure what to make of Lilian's dreamy demeanor.

Lilian giggled and then did something completely unexpected. She took Morgana by the hand and led her in a promenade all around the room. Morgana tried to wriggle loose, but Lilian only held more tightly and smiled more gleefully. Morgana found herself smiling back, though more out of embarrassment and discomfort than enjoyment. She had never learned to dance properly, and she felt wholly out of step with Lilian's joyful spirit.

"Have mercy, and let me be!" she begged at last.

"Just one more turn," Lilian pressed.

But Morgana broke free. She could not indulge

such foolishness, even for Lilian. "I do believe you are touched. What has come over you?"

"Perhaps I am touched! It is just that I sense something magnificent is about to happen. I feel as though everything I have ever dreamed of is about to come true," Lilian beamed. "I am sorry I upset you yesterday with talk of the new king. I was so relieved to find you in better spirits when you came back from your outing. Was it not wonderful of Lancelot to call upon us?"

"Indeed, it was," Morgana replied, masking her heavy heart. Then, glancing at a parchment on the table, she commented, "Pray, what is this? Are you working on a new design for a tapestry?"

"Oh yes! This one will be the most beautiful *and* the most tragic of them all."

Morgana looked over the sketch. Though far from complete, it showed the silhouette of a knight kneeling before an altar aglow with light. His hands were cast upward in a defensive posture, and his shoulders shrunk down low as if in distress.

"What troubles him?" Morgana asked.

"His sins," Lilian replied. "Or should I say, 'sin.' He is a great knight who has fallen from grace because of committing the grave sin of adultery and betraying his lord in the process."

Morgana turned ghostly pale and looked up from the tapestry into Lilian's shining eyes.

"Love, what inspired such a scandalous story? It is so unlike your other designs."

Lilian blushed and lowered her eyes. She had

not expected Morgana to take issue with the illicit nature of the story and suddenly felt the need to defend her character. "Do not fret so, Aunt. It is just a story." When her words were met with silence, she added, "I am not a little girl anymore. I know that life is full of heartache as well as joy. It is just as you said all those years ago, 'Art must depict life as it is, not as we would have it.'"

Morgana was stunned to learn Lilian had remembered her words.

"Besides, I have been pondering this story for as long as I can remember. Grandmother and I made it up together," Lilian added.

This was a revelation indeed.

"Did Grandmother help you make up your other stories?" Morgana inquired, hoping to gain insight into the source of Lilian's visions. Never had their prophetic nature been discussed between them. Indeed, Lilian seemed naively unaware of her gift.

"Oh, no, just this one. Sometimes she would begin the yarn; at others, I would. We told it so often for a time that I can hardly remember where her ideas ended and mine began. I suppose it all became one," Lilian mused. "She knew I was young for such scandalous talk, but she said I needed to take caution from it."

"Caution?" Morgana asked.

"Yes," Lilian laughed. "Grandmother would say, 'Men are not always what they seem.' She worried I was too innocent."

"Grandmother was so full of wisdom and insight,"

Morgana replied in a half-teasing, half-serious sort of way, but feeling firm at last in her decision to separate Lilian and Lancelot. There could be no doubt Grandmother would have done the same.

At nightfall, once Lilian was fast asleep, Morgana slipped out to call on Eloise. When she arrived, her sad eyes rested on the cottage, and she thought of all that had come to pass since her first encounter with that cursed place. She had changed much since that time. In her early years, she had sunk so deep into the darkness that she reveled in her visits with Eloise. Now, after having allowed the light of Grandmother's affections to flicker in her dim heart, she abhorred the thought of what lay ahead. She reluctantly raised her hand to knock on the door, but it swung open before she even so much as grazed it with her knuckles.

"Welcome home, Morgana," Eloise called from a back room.

Two steaming cups of tea sat on the table.

"Prithee, take a seat and enjoy your tea. I will join you presently."

Morgana felt a chill in her body as the cat slinked around her legs and drew her into the chair. She needed to calm her nerves. She clasped one of the mugs and tried to absorb its warmth. As she did, Eloise emerged carrying a leather-bound book with an unusual pattern emblazoned on the cover. Morgana had never seen the book before.

"I made it just how you like it—or at least how you used to like it. Neither too strong nor too blashy, with a little cream and sugar." Eloise nodded toward the tea as she laid the heavy book on the table.

"Grammarcy," Morgana replied politely, though she cared only for its warmth.

"Before we get started, I want to set your mind at ease—if I can," Eloise began in her crackly voice. "I fear you have come to think ill of me, that you have come to question my intent all these years." Eloise paused for effect. She had rehearsed everything in advance. "My dear Morgana, I am as much a victim of Fate as you. I was happy living a life of solitude, but then you showed up at my cottage, scared and desperate for help. Even so cold-hearted a person as I could not help but take pity on you. I saw the sad life behind you and before you all in an instant, and I knew you needed a friend, a mentor…a mother. Prithee, believe me when I say that I have always sought to help you find happiness. If it were in my power, I would have freed you from your quest long ago. Such as it is, I want nothing but to bring you, and even those whom you care about, safely through to its completion. Rest assured the end is within sight."

A mother?

Morgana's eyes were cast downward. She was weary from the many years of carrying such a heavy emotional load, and she could not bear to have more guilt thrust upon her. It was true that Eloise had been a mentor and even a sort of friend, but Morgana had never thought of her as a mother. Indeed, none had been able to fill that role in her life. But she wondered if it was possible Eloise had thought of Morgana as a daughter.

"There is no need to respond. I just needed you to hear me out," Eloise continued. Indeed, Eloise did not want to engage the subject further. She simply wanted to win back Morgana's confidence enough to move forward.

"The only one I have come to doubt is myself. Now, tell me what I ought to do," Morgana replied, still avoiding eye contact.

"Very well, then." Eloise's lips curved into a smile as she flipped through the book. Its mysterious, illuminated script and aged parchment crinkled with every turn of the page. "Ah, here it is—the dream lover spell. One so deeply in love as Lilian could not bear separation from the object of her affection without a little help. This is a gentle spell, for a heart in love is delicate. It will whisk Lilian away to an enchanted tower on the Island of Shalott, safe from the false love of Lancelot. She will live there alone as though in a dream and forget all about him."

Anticipating protest over Lilian living in isolation, Eloise raised her hand and continued, "Rest assured, she will live not only in comfort but in pleasure, for she will live out her calling as an artist. Day after day, she will look down upon Camelot through a magical mirror and weave its wondrous sights into the most beautiful tapestry the world has ever known. Though she will live as if in a dream, she will see more than ever she hath imagined in her little wooded cottage. When the spell expires and she awakens, Lancelot will be a shadow of the past, a mere figment of her imagination. His betrayal will hurt King Arthur alone."

"What will become of her other memories?" Morgana asked. She was worried Lilian would forget her, too.

"They will be intact—mostly. Only those which relate to Lancelot will vanish," Eloise replied. Sensing Morgana's disappointment, she added, "It is but a small price to pay for Lilian's protection."

"And how long will it last?" asked Morgana.

"It will expire on its own the day after Lilian turns sixteen," replied Eloise.

"It is such a long time…"

"So it must be to keep Lilian safe. In the interim, Lancelot will pledge fealty to King Arthur and gain the favor of the queen—remember, he would do that whether Lilian is in the picture or not."

Relaxing her hands at last from their tight grip around the mug, Morgana pulled the book toward her and studied the spell for herself. It was all there just as Eloise had said. Still she asked, "Is there no other way?"

"I wish there were," Eloise replied.

The sincerity in her voice was so unlike her usual callousness. Morgana looked up at her directly and studied her countenance. That was when she noticed a faint cloudiness in Eloise's once luminous eyes. Her face had lost whatever fullness and vigor it had once had. Her entire bearing looked weak.

"My health is failing, Morgana," Eloise said dryly in response to Morgana's inquisitive stare. "Let an old woman make amends for a life of darkness by doing something good."

Eloise held out her hand, and Morgana gave it a slight, clammy squeeze, scooped up the book, and took leave of the cottage.

4

The sun was just rising over the horizon when Morgana got home. She entered silently, hoping not to awaken Lilian, but it was too late. The young woman was already busy with morning chores. They stood, staring at one another in awkward silence. Lilian appeared fresh as the morning dew. Morgana stood a dark shadow. She could cast off the hand of Fate no longer.

"Pray! Where have you been off to at such an early hour?" Lilian asked uneasily. Something was obviously wrong.

"Lilian," Morgana began, ignoring the question, "my heart has been heavy with fear for your well-being. I know you cannot understand, but... what I do is out of love."

"Your words trouble me. Prithee, sit and rest, dear Aunt," Lilian replied.

Morgana looked at her lovingly and began mumbling something under her breath and raising her arms slowly. It appeared she was calling for an embrace, and Lilian instinctively stepped toward her. How trusting she was! As Lilian came closer, she heard:

> *Willows whiten, aspens quiver,*
> *Little breezes dusk and shiver*
> *Through the wave that runs forever*
> *By the island in the river,*
> > *Flowing down to Camelot.*
> *Four gray walls, and four gray towers,*
> *Overlook a space of flowers,*
> *And the silent isle embowers*
> > *The Lady of Shalott...*

Lilian grew faint, lost consciousness, and stumbled right into Morgana's trembling arms. Unsteady though they were, Morgana cradled her like a baby all the way to Grandmother's rickety old carriage. Memories of their first journey together, when Lilian was but a newborn fresh from the womb, filled Morgana's thoughts. Then, as now, she wanted nothing more than to keep Lilian safe. She hoped with all her heart the tower would afford the same protection Grandmother's cottage had offered. Only this time, there would be no one to greet Morgana, no one in whom she could entrust Lilian's care. Morgana felt sad, lonely, and tired. Worse yet, she was plagued by doubts—doubts about herself, her motives, and her sincerity. Did she sense what truly lay ahead? Did she somehow know all would not be as she was told? No matter the answer, Morgana was in a terrible state. The weight of her responsibility hung all around like a shroud and grew thicker and thicker until she felt like she could hardly breathe.

When the carriage finally stopped, Morgana looked out across the river to the tiny island there in the middle—the Island of Shalott. In the early afternoon sun, its solitary tower stood proud against the blue sky, and groves of lilies danced all around it. To any but Morgana, it would have appeared a beautiful sight, almost romantic in its mysterious desolation. So sad was she in her task, however, all she saw was a forsaken crypt.

Under normal circumstances, rowing the half-mile to the island would have been pleasurable exercise. As it was, Morgana was simply too drained to continue on without the help of her powers. With great effort, she flipped her hand this way and that, magically transporting Lilian from the carriage to the boat and setting sail. It was an easy voyage, nonetheless, short and swift. The wind swept them across the current in one long breath. When they ran aground, Morgana flipped her hand yet again, rousing an unconscious Lilian to her feet.

"Be not afraid, Love," Morgana whispered as they approached the tower. "It may look lonely, but you will be safe inside yonder walls."

Morgana's heart sank still further when her words were met with complete silence. Lilian could not hear Morgana nor was she even aware of her presence. The spell had indeed taken hold of the young lady. Though Lilian never faltered in her step, she walked like one in a deep sleep, her vacant eyes fixed on a door at the base of the tower. Indeed, she knew exactly where to go and quickened her step in earnest the closer she got. Lilian opened the door and began ascending a high passage of stairs with Morgana close at her heels. Around and around the women climbed, neither stopping to rest, until the passage spilled out into a large, lavishly furnished room. Lilian seated herself before a loom and instantly began weaving.

Morgana, breathless from the climb, could not bear the sight of Lilian, her beautiful ward, niece, and friend, her one true companion, working the warp strings in a lifeless stupor. Gently touching the back of her hand to Lilian's cheek, she said, "All the world is at your fingertips, even if you know it not, and, when you awake, the world will be a safer place…Until anon."

There was nothing more to say, so Morgana turned to leave. Suddenly a thought flashed through her mind. She recalled the fabric Grandmother had purchased for Lilian on her thirteenth birthday. It had remained untouched since then, gathering dust in the bureau. Perhaps the time had finally come to turn it into a gown for Lilian. At least in that small way, though unknowingly, Lilian could feel the tender warmth of those who loved her.

Gentle muses, timeless style,
Dress this girl in fine attire.

Instantly, Lilian wore a gorgeous blue dress more beautiful than Morgana could have imagined. Smiling sadly, Morgana left.

When Lancelot arrived at Grandmother's cottage to ask for Lilian's hand in marriage, he was utterly dismayed to find no trace of either her or Morgana. Another would have turned away believing himself rejected, but not Lancelot. He sought news in town and at the monastery, but no one knew anything about their disappearance. Confusion gave way to fear and eventually anger as he labored to find out where they had gone and what could have happened. He felt certain of Lilian's love for him and was convinced evil forces were afoot. Heartbroken and headstrong, he set out across the Realm of Logres in search of his love.

Lilian would have ached to know how he suffered. Always in a state of unconsciousness, however, she knew nothing of his plight nor did she even think of him. She knew not whether she was awake or asleep, and it did not matter, for the time passed as if it were one continuous day.

She watched the world go by through a mirror that hung opposite the tower window. In that manner, she saw all that passed without ever looking through the window directly—indeed the spell prohibited her to look out of it. She did not know the difference, however, and dreamily wove its magnificent sights into a never-ending tapestry. She would see the mundane as well as the sublime. Sometimes she would see an abbot on an ambling pad or a curly shepherd lad tending sheep in the pastures. At others, she would lament the passing of a funeral procession or rejoice at the sight of a magnificent wedding party. She captured every sight in her tapestry with a beauty and grace beyond her natural powers. As she worked, her voice in song would carry through the breeze, over the river, and down to Camelot.

But we 'twas poisoned with the dark of night…

So beautiful was the sound, that the townspeople came to believe a fairy had graced the realm. Only Morgana knew differently. She would shudder at the sound of Lilian's voice floating through the air. It was a poisoned arrow shot straight through her. Convinced as she was of the soundness of her actions, her heart said otherwise. If only she had listened to it, perhaps she could have found a way to undo all the damage she had unwittingly done.

Part V

To Camelot

Had I the crude and scrannel rhymes to suit
the melancholy hole upon which all
the other circling crags converge and rest,
the juice of my conception would be pressed
more fully; but because I feel their lack,
I bring myself to speak, yet speak in fear;
for it is not a task to take in jest,
to show the base of all the universe—
nor for a tongue that cries out, "mama," "papa."

- DANTE ALIGHIERI, *THE DIVINE COMEDY*,
CANTO XXXII, VERSES 1-9

1

As the seasons of the year changed and Morgana impatiently waited for the spell to expire, she went about in a hooded cloak, garnering whatever information she could find out about King Arthur. Though she sought to sully his character and justify her vendetta, he appeared always morally upright and stainless. The entire kingdom loved him and respected him as if he were their own blood. Nevertheless, she scoffed at word of his valor in battle and righteousness in rule. She dismissed his noble reputation as the idle chatter of a people desperate for someone to lead them against the Saxons. And when news reached her of Arthur's upcoming marriage on the Feast of Pentecost to the beautiful, gray-eyed Lady Guinevere, Morgana laughed most callously.

"What a pathetic fool!" she pronounced bitterly. "I must see the 'happy' couple for myself."

When the day of the wedding arrived, Morgana approached the grand pavilion like any other guest, only she veiled herself in obscurity. She traded out her cloak for a simple velvet gown in black midnight and wore her hair in a long, ribboned braid down her back, as was the fashion. Under different circumstances, she may have enjoyed getting dressed up and may have gone to great lengths to embellish her remaining assets. As it was, she sought only to blend in. Lacking in luster, she walked past the guards unnoticed and settled into anonymity.

You must be more careful, Younger Brother! Though the kingdom may sing your praises, I sense a note of dissonance. Perhaps you believe yourself invincible. Uther certainly did.

Just then, a knight approached Morgana with hand on hilt. "I do not believe I have made your acquaintance."

Morgana spied him up and down, noting his silvery black hair and strong frame. He had a glint of combat about his person, but it was impossible to take him seriously. He looked like one playing the part of a knight.

"No, you have not," she declared hotly. "And I dare say you shall not with such an impertinent manner."

"Forgive me, I prithee," he replied taken aback, quickly moving his hand off the hilt and offering it to Morgana in courtly fashion. "My name is Sir Urien. I—I am not particularly good at social conventions."

"I should say not," replied Morgana curtly, though her heart was touched with sympathy. In truth she felt every bit as awkward as he looked.

"I simply meant to make your acquaintance," he fumbled.

He was neither handsome nor charming, but

she would have welcomed his attentions had she the liberty to enjoy them. Instead, she whispered:

Merry melodies, sweet libations,
Send away this man's temptations.

In an instant, Sir Urien disappeared back into the crowd, forgetting—for the time—his failed attempt to learn Morgana's name. Free once again from distraction, she looked on at the banquet.

There was music and dancing and feasting beyond any Morgana had ever experienced. Damsels promenaded coyly with knights, no doubt wishing to land a match themselves. Pages brought out tray after tray of the finest meats—boar, mutton, venison, pork, and poultry—all richly displayed with choice fruits and vegetables. The sound of goblets clashing adorned the music of the troubadours, who performed in every corner of the great hall. As Morgana's eyes moved from the dance floor to the banquet tables, scanning for the king and queen, she spied a round table larger and more finely garnished than the rest. Nearly every seat was filled with a handsome knight.

A-ha! she nearly said aloud. *But where is the head? How ever is one to know who is in charge?*

Truly, there was no way of discerning the king and queen save for the crowns on their heads. Morgana spotted Guinevere first, for she was richly clad in a gown made of golden silk to match her golden hair. She was a breathtaking sight. Graceful yet reserved, she exuded royalty without the customary haughtiness. Even Morgana, one set on disliking the queen, could not deny her beauty.

But does she love Arthur?

The incline of her head, the slant of her shoulders—everything about her body language—was directed toward the king. She was a picture of nuptial bliss. Perhaps Morgana was too swayed by her knowledge of the future to judge fairly, but she detected something amiss in the queen's gray eyes, something distant and guarded, a far-off longing. None but Morgana noticed the look. Indeed, she may have imagined it, but Morgana's anger flared up just the same.

Temptress!

Morgana thought of the queen's imminent hand in turning Lancelot's head. She thought, too, of Lilian, imprisoned on the Island of Shalott, unable to face the woman who would steal away her true love. Morgana thought of her own drab appearance and the toll the quests had taken on her marriage prospects. She thought of all that could have been. She thought of Sir Urien…

Anyone would look beauteous clad in so fine a dress. But none would be more so than Lilian.

Her jealousy stoked, Morgana examined next her half-brother, Arthur. He wore a majestic red cloak trimmed with ermine atop a belted white tunic bearing the seal of the House of Pendragon. His face bore a strong familial resemblance. He had the same dignified nose as their mother. Touching her own, Morgana realized they shared it in common. Indeed, they resembled one another quite remarkably in facial structure, save for their brows. Arthur's was proud and strong just as Uther's had been, only a touch gentler. By his manner, it was obvious he adored his new wife. He doted on her as much as was befitting a young king—offering his hand, smiling, and whispering in her ear. Morgana was sickened by his display of affection, not least because she started to feel bad for him, and that was not something she would permit herself.

As she had anticipated, her own mother sat on Arthur's other side. She looked becoming as usual, dressed in an exquisite gown and bejeweled more than the queen herself. Morgana stiffened and smoothed the folds of her skirt as she watched Igraine play the part of the queen mother, beaming with pride. Never in all her life had Igraine paid half as much attention to Morgana as she paid Arthur. The worst part was that Igraine did not seem to be pretending. Her affections appeared wholly sincere and natural. Morgana felt green with envy.

Would you had looked on me half as lovingly. All may have been different, but instead, you sent me away....Now you will lose us both.

Morgana felt more abandoned and alone than ever, orphaned though one parent yet lived and stood before her. She noted the empty seat beside her mother's.

And where has your newest suitor gone off to?

"The seat is reserved for the king's half-sister," observed a mysterious, older gentleman with a long gray beard and a gray robe to match.

"Pardon?" Morgana replied taken aback. She had not spoken her thought aloud.

"The empty seat next to the queen mother—it is reserved for the king's half-sister, the Lady Morgana," continued the stranger. "His majesty has eagerly sought her acquaintance but without success. It is said she had a falling out with her mother, but it must have been far worse than the rumors tell or surely she would have come hither for the royal wedding."

"Perhaps she is ill or deceased," Morgana commented flippantly. She was anxious to be rid of the chatty stranger.

He moved in closer. "Perhaps...but that does not explain why her cottage was boarded up when the king's herald went to deliver the invitation. His men could find no trace of her despite an exhaustive search...Do you want to know what I think happened?" The man lowered his voice. "I think she has been bewitched."

What utter nonsense!

Even more vexed, Morgana knew not how to respond, but there was no need. Conversation throughout the entire banquet hall came to an abrupt halt as everyone's attention turned to a most unusual raucous. A white hart had come running full speed into the banquet hall with a small white brachet nipping fiercely at its heels. Around and around they ran, clearing the dance floor and knocking into more than one page balancing heavy serving trays over their heads. Food spilled everywhere.

The women were aghast at the mayhem and squeamish about ruining their beautiful gowns, but King Arthur and his knights laughed uproariously at the sight—that is, all but one named Sir Abelleus. He flew into a rage when his surcoat got soiled from a spill, seized the brachet with his brawny hands, and ran off with it, no doubt planning to do it ill. His outburst was met with all manner of exclamations. Some continued laughing for they saw sport in their comrade's embarrassment. Others chastised the knight for being too sensitive and brash.

Moments later, a fair damsel on a white palfrey came riding into the banquet, and a hush came over the crowd as all waited to hear her speak. Surely, some strange enchantment was afoot. "My Lord," she began, addressing King Arthur, "yonder crazed knight has stolen off with my brachet. I implore you to pursue him and bring back what is rightfully mine."

King Arthur rose and stood upright. At well over six feet, his commanding presence quickly brought the entire hall to their knees. Morgana bowed deeply as well, but kept her eyes raised so as not to miss a thing. Lilian's dream was coming true before her very eyes.

"Right truly would I, but today is a day like none other. The realm has been graced with a queen. By my own order, the entire kingdom has pledged to celebrate in her honor and forswear quests, no matter their nature."

Morgana looked from Arthur to Guinevere, the

latter of whom blushed faintly and tugged on her husband's sleeve.

"Then woe to you and the queen," the damsel replied. "Better to honor your wife by honoring all women in need than to hold your kingdom hostage in her name."

"Hold your tongue—" the king started at her insolent remark, but a familiar voice cut him off. It was the strange fellow whom Morgana had wanted to be rid of.

"Sire, there is wisdom in her words even if they are unkindly spoken. Let not your wedding day be marked with the shame of refusing help to a damsel in distress."

"My good friend and advisor, Merlin, I will follow your sage counsel," the king replied in softer tones.

Just then, another knight rode into the hall, hoisted the unsuspecting damsel onto his horse most disrespectfully, and rode away, with her panting and fighting all the while. It happened so suddenly and followed such a bizarre sequence of events, none had the wherewithal to stop it. The young king looked greatly disturbed as he surveyed the mess that had been made of his wedding banquet. He had hoped for a respite from the troubles that plagued his kingdom, just one day to enjoy life frivolously, but such was not his lot. Though he had much still to learn of being a king, he knew his responsibility was always first to the realm. It had been a foolhardy notion to forswear his duties for the day, but he had done it innocently enough. Looking at his beautiful bride, Arthur stood more confidently and began giving orders to right the wrongs that had been committed.

"None shall suffer to be injured without recourse in the Realm of Logres, which shall hereafter be known as the Realm of Righteousness," he proclaimed to cheers.

Queen Guinevere beamed, and Merlin, the Good Enchanter nodded approvingly. Having learned what she set out to, Morgana stole a glance at Sir Urien. He, too, was sullied by the mess but seemed either unaware or unconcerned. Morgana shook her head disparagingly, turned to leave, and noticed Lancelot's name emblazed on one of the empty seats at the round table.

Lancelot shall pledge fealty to King Arthur soon... Eloise spoke truly.

Morgana was filled with bitter relief. But what did she make of Arthur? Did she find him deserving of her wrath? Was he a fitting proxy for the vengeance she sought on Uther? She left feeling neither vindicated right nor proven wrong. Clearly, Arthur was young and rash, but nevertheless, he seemed upright in his intentions, guided as they were by Merlin.

Fate has abused us both, Younger Brother. Morgana brushed her palms across her skirt and reminded herself that Arthur had freely chosen his bride for himself. *May you find the means to cast off her hand.*

2

Morgana played back the details of the wedding banquet over and over again. There was so much to ponder, to question, to dream about....

She thought most of Merlin and his seemingly infinite powers. Did he know whom he had been talking to? He must have! So what did he mean when he said Morgana was bewitched? Was he mocking her, or was he actually trying to deliver some cryptic message? Then there was Arthur and her mother. Had they really wished her present at the wedding? If they did, surely it was for the sake of the family image and not out of a desire to kindle the family bond. Sometimes Morgana would think of Sir Urien, and her lips would curl into a smile. What else might he have said if she had permitted the conversation to continue? Morgana liked indulging his memory best of all, even though she thought him wanting in charm and knew it was for naught, anyway. Then there was the white hart, the brachet, and the mysterious damsel, crashing the banquet just as Lilian's story had long ago, unknowingly foretold. Such was yet another reminder, a reassurance, that Lilian's prophecies were true, that separating her from Lancelot had been the right thing to do.

When all but a day remained before Lilian's sixteenth birthday, sad and forlorn, she ventured back to Grandmother's cottage to make ready for Lilian's return and assume a semblance of normalcy. Its boarded windows and door seemed to chide her for having been abandoned so many months. Never had it known anything but joy and hospitality in its many long years, and now it was wrought with cobwebs and musk.

She cleaned the cottage with a critical eye and a loving hand, preferring not to use her magic. It felt good to use her muscles and feel them warm with wholesome work. She talked to the cottage as if it were an old friend.

"I prithee, do not look at me like that...I did what I had to...The time apart has been hard on all of us, but things will be better now...Of course she will be back, too...No, *he* is not welcome anymore..."

Once she had unboarded the main floor and given it a thorough sweep and wash, she ventured upstairs. Her first task was to open the windows and let the fresh air blow away the musty smell. She then set about sorting her personal effects, which she had neglected to organize in her hasty departure. With a tinge of guilt, she scooped up Grandmother's Rosary beads, which she had carelessly dropped on the floor that fateful night, and placed them in her pocket. Just as she began stripping the bedding, a strong gust of wind swept through the room, nearly tearing the linens from her hands. When the wind subsided, Morgana saw a torrent of parchment strewn across the floor.

"Why, these must have come from Lilian's room. They look like her drawings," she mused aloud.

She picked up one drawing and then another glancing at each as she went. At first, she was simply impressed with the drawings, casually noting Lilian's graceful lines and dramatic tones, but then she realized the drawings were nearly all variants of two scenes. One showed a handsome young couple standing before the altar with their hands locked in the Sacrament of Holy Matrimony. The man wore a shining suit of armor swept up in a gallant cloak, and the woman wore a beautiful blue gown with a long, elegant train that looked like a sky of roses. Soft halos shone about their bowed heads as an archbishop prayed above them, blessing them with the Sign of the Cross.

The other scene made Morgana's heart sink. It showed an old woman standing before an enormous mirror and weaving an endless tapestry. Her gown was as worn as her face was dull and lifeless. Two disembodied eyes hovered above the scene looking at everything. The eyes, cloudy and sinister, were unmistakably Eloise's.

Whether consciously or not, Lilian had drawn her own future. Only, the scenes did not match

Eloise's prediction. Lilian was not to be happily married nor was she to be imprisoned in the tower indefinitely. It did not make any sense unless Eloise was somehow wrong.

"Which vision is correct?" Morgana considered aloud, more perplexed than ever.

There could be no doubt a threat remained on Lilian's life, but was it really a threat from Lancelot after all? Her body stiffened as she considered where else the threat could lie; she could think of none other than Eloise, the orchestrator of everything since Lilian's birth. Morgana looked out the window and realized the sun was already sinking low on the horizon. She needed to get to Lilian as fast as she could and keep watch through her sixteenth birthday. Once the day of the threat was over, she would ensure the spell was undone.

Morgana set out at once in Grandmother's carriage and cried:

Forcefields gather, elements scatter,
Draw this carriage onward faster!

On and on she raced. The journey felt endless. Her heart quickened to the rhythm of the horse's hooves, and she felt her veins contract and expand as the blood coursed through and warmed her body to the tips. She began to perspire even though the night air was cool, and Morgana realized she had never been so worried. She tugged the reins harder and faster, but she refused to give in to the feeling of panic that seemed to press in from all sides. If she had learned anything from Eloise's tutelage, it was that moments of urgency must be met with calm and control.

Morgana sighed in relief when, at last, she made it to the river's edge and uncovered the boat she had hidden among the bramble. It had remained untouched since she had taken Lilian to the Island of Shalott in the first place. As she hurriedly flipped the boat over and began dragging it to the water, she suddenly stopped. Was it her imagination, or did she hear the quiet shuffle of footsteps? She waited. The sound vanished, but Morgana knew someone or something was in her midst. She stretched out her fingers and breathed deeply, trying to discern what it could be, but she could not get a scent. It was not that Morgana was out of practice, though she was, but that she was out of her league. Taking on the wolf pack three years back was child's play compared to what stalked her that day. Morgana stepped silently away from the boat and began to survey the area with her eyes. As she turned a half-step to the right, she saw a dark image.

"Eloise!" Morgana gasped, and then everything went black.

When Morgana awoke, she found herself imprisoned in a stone cell with scant light but for the morning sun that squeezed through a few small cracks. Morgana's head throbbed, and not only from the large gash upon it. So too it hurt from the pain of trying over and again to understand something beyond her grasp. Reeling with confusion, she forced herself onto her feet and tried to regain composure. She closed her eyes and breathed deeply, conjuring her powers, but none came. She opened her eyes and examined her hands in utter stupefaction. Perhaps she needed to regain better composure. She closed her eyes and meditated for a long time. Again, she raised her hands and called on her powers. Nothing. She was somehow struck powerless.

The realization of her utter helplessness was too much for her. Morgana's mind flashed back to the death of her father. She could once again see his lifeless, shrouded body lowered into the grave. She could hear her own desperate pleas to bring him back. She could see her mother turning away emotionless, deaf to her agonizing cries. All her past and present suffering swelled together in one painful deluge. Morgana squeezed her head tightly and screamed, letting go of every bit of calm and control she had left. She clawed at the walls and called for help until she was too hoarse to continue. Sobbing, she fell to her knees and began pounding on her lap. That was when she felt Grandmother's Rosary in her pocket.

Morgana pulled it out and wove it through her fingers. Then cautiously, she held the crucifix between her thumb and forefingers and made the Sign of the Cross. She spoke no intentions, but a call for help was ever in her heart as she recited the prayers of the Holy Rosary countless times through. With each utterance, she gained deeper and deeper acceptance of her weakness. She prayed for humility; she prayed for fortitude; most of all, she prayed for forgiveness. When she finally finished, she heard a whisper.

Suffering is the path to redemption.

Something stirred within Morgana's heart, and a new feeling of hope took hold. She bowed low, and the words to break the spell, words of wisdom and virtue, came to her:

Willows whiten, aspens quiver,
Sleeping heart now dusk and shiver,
Let true love float down the river,
  Skimming down to Lancelot.
And when the sun is overhead,
Knowing now true love's not dead,
Send him forth to save and wed,
  The Lady of Shalott.

3

Little did Morgana know Lilian was just above her, dreamily weaving away. As the words were spoken, the younger woman felt love stir within her, and she began to gaze at the images flashing across the mirror with longing eyes. Still in an altered state, she knew not what she was looking for, but her heart, too, was full of hope. She suddenly became conscious of time and felt impatient with the task before her. She wove faster and faster as if she could make the scene for which she was waiting appear more quickly. Her anticipation grew with each long minute until all at once she saw a knight riding in her direction on the other side of the river. Her hands ceased their mechanical weaving, and she peered more closely into the mirror. The knight rode atop a white horse bedazzled with jewels on the bridle, outshone only by his golden hair and radiant countenance.

"I know him," she said, still not fully conscience. "I must take a better look." So turning from the mirror, she approached the forbidden window, rested her arms on the ledge, and swooned, "Lancelot!"

Just as she did, thunder cracked in the cloudless sky, and an angry wind blew through the tower, shattering the mirror and whisking the tapestry away into thin air. Still dazed from the trance, Lilian did not understand what was happening, but she rightly sensed imminent danger. She looked about for an exit and found an open door leading to a staircase. She descended as quickly as she could, but her strength waned with every step. Her body was failing her just as her mind was recovering. She stumbled out of the tower and into the storm. Scanning, she saw the very boat Morgana had prepared waiting at bay. It took her last bit of energy to board the boat and send it adrift down the river headed toward Camelot. She desperately looked for Lancelot along the shore, but she could see little through the metal, pounding rain.

Alas! Lilian's brave knight had already turned for cover. Though Morgana's words had drawn him out, he sensed nothing of Lilian's presence let alone her dire state. Doubt had taken hold of him during his year-long search for Lilian, and his heart had grown numb to true love's call. He was no longer a man brimming with hope, but one weakened by heartache and despair.

As the storm raged outside, the voice in Morgana's cell grew louder and louder in refrain.

Suffering is the path to redemption…

Fueled by its words, Morgana paced around the cell and pushed on every stone, desperate for a way out. Magically, a door appeared where there had been none, and she was able to walk right through it, out into the elements—only, she was too late. Lilian was already floating down the river. Morgana ran as fast as she could through the muddy terrain, trying in vain to use her powers, but they still would not come. She yelled out, frantically calling Lilian to stop, but her voice was lost in the rain. She had no way of catching Lilian. The best she could hope for was to swim from the island to the opposite shore and run after the boat as it drifted.

Scared, Morgana waded into the treacherous water but stopped. Attempting to swim was madness—there was no way she would make it without her powers. Then all of a sudden, the storm turned to a gentle rain, and the rough waters became still. Morgana dove forward, taking advantage of the reprieve. The icy water chilled her down to the bone. Though her arms pulled hard and her legs kicked constantly, her body refused to warm up. She shivered as she swam and swallowed water with every breath. She tried to swim a straight line to the opposite shore, but the current led her askew. She was stuck, unable to overcome the powerful rapid. She held tightly to Grandmother's Rosary as the water swallowed her, tossed her about, and miraculously spit her up on the other side. Words thundered in the sky.

Suffering is the path to redemption!

Morgana pulled herself onto her feet and tried to run, but she could not get any traction in the slippery mud and found herself sliding about.

Though the little boat was no longer in sight, it could not be too far ahead—or so Morgana thought. She prayed it would run ashore. She continued as quickly as she could, looking for Lilian around every bend, but she was nowhere to be seen. She became hopeful when the rain finally stopped altogether, but her hope gave way to desperation as she trudged further and further unsuccessfully.

"Enough!" a gentle voice commanded finally. A tall, beautiful woman who looked neither old nor young appeared out of nowhere and stood before Morgana. "You have suffered enough for now. You must not pursue Lilian any further."

Outraged at the stranger's intrusion, Morgana demanded hoarsely, "Out of my way!"

"You have nothing to fear, Morgana," the woman replied tenderly. She touched Morgana's bloodied head, and the gash healed instantly. "Lilian is safe now."

"I do not understand. Where is she?" Morgana questioned as muddy tears streamed down her hot face.

"She is in the Vale of Avalon. In time, you will be able to join her, but you must first make amends for your wrongdoings. You have sinned greatly throughout your quest. Though it has been through evil guidance, you still bear the responsibility for your actions," the woman continued. "Your prayer in the tower cell was only the beginning. Much still needs to be done if you are to achieve redemption, and, I am afraid, some things cannot be reversed."

"How do you know all this?" Morgana asked, touching her head where the gash had been. "Who are you?"

"I am the Lady Nimue," she replied.

Morgana stood aghast. Long had she desired the acquaintance of Nimue. Now, standing in her very presence, healed by her hand, Morgana realized the truth of Nimue's greatness far surpassed her reputation. Lady Nimue was goodness and beauty, wisdom and grace itself.

"I want to see Lilian…" Morgana pleaded helplessly.

"In time. For now, you must content yourself with my word that she is safe," Nimue replied. "You must now receive the direction you so oft needed. You were wrong in trusting Eloise—it is she who misled you all these years, though you were more than willing to be blinded by her in your unrighteous quest for vengeance and thirst for power. Such is the way of evil. It preys on our weaknesses and makes false promises."

"But why? Why would Eloise mislead me?" Morgana asked.

"Like so many others drawn to the dark, Eloise is driven by an unquenchable thirst for power. Injury to you and Lilian was but a trivial matter. She sought something that only one with a pure heart such as Lilian could see. For that reason, she needed to see the world through Lilian's eyes," Nimue explained. "Eloise hoped the tapestry Lilian wove would reveal that which she sought most."

"What of the prophecies? Of the threats? Were those all contrived by Eloise?" Morgana asked.

"Not exactly," Nimue began. "The threats were real, but Eloise manipulated the third one—and you—to her advantage. She led you to believe that the black arts were the means of securing a happy future, but the truth was really quite the opposite. Lilian's goodness had secured her a happy future with Lancelot. There was nothing standing in the way of that save you."

"Does that mean *I* was the third and final threat?" Morgana asked incredulously.

"In a manner of speaking, yes. It is through your heavy hand, though falsely guided by Eloise, that Lilian nearly got stuck in the tower forever," Nimue stated. "Do not look so forlorn, though. You are also to thank for her freedom. Had you not recognized the error of your spell, Lilian would not now be safe in the Vale of Avalon."

"Can she be reunited with Lancelot?" Morgana asked with a glimmer of hope.

"I fear not," Nimue replied wistfully. "Lancelot has this very day joined the court of King Arthur."

"What will become of him?" Morgana asked meekly, recalling the maternal role Lady Nimue had played in his upbringing.

Nimue replied sadly, "Without Lilian by his side, he will follow a perilous path."

"It is all my fault," Morgana said, cradling her head in her arms.

"It is true you brought about their separation,

but he is responsible for his future just as you are responsible for your own," Nimue explained. "And those with a pure heart like Lilian will always have a chance at love."

Morgana's heart fluttered as hope began to spring anew. *Perhaps I, too…*

Nimue smiled as if she knew Morgana's secret pining.

"What of Arthur?" Morgana asked with downcast eyes.

"It is one thing to plot another's destruction, and quite another to carry it out. Is it not?"

Morgana could not look up. The words cut deeply as she realized how recklessly she had longed for revenge, never knowing the true cost of her desire, never realizing it would be without satisfaction. "Then it is done? His downfall is now inevitable?"

"Perhaps—but you may help your brother yet. While you cannot change what is done," Nimue explained, "you can move forward with a new quest, one infused with greater power than you have so far known, power forged in goodness and truth."

Weary at such a thought, Morgana could barely utter, "What kind of quest?"

Nimue replied, "A quest for virtue. A quest to bring about the glory of Logres. Embrace the light your grandmother—and your father—wished for you, and you shall be successful. Great was their suffering on earth, and great is their eternal reward. So may it be for you."

As Lady Nimue imparted more wisdom, the

luminous faces of her father and grandmother appeared before her and spoke in once voice.

Love others as we have loved you...

Morgana listened with sorrow and regret, but not the kind tainted by self-pity that she had been prone to her whole life. Instead, she accepted her lot and owned her actions. She would embrace the light. She would make amends. She would start again, come what may.

Epilogue

Morgana bravely marched forth to Eloise's cottage. As she crossed the threshold, she expected the door to swing open on its own as it had always done in the past, but it did not. She turned the handle and walked in unannounced. The table was bare, the rocking chair empty, the cat nowhere. Indeed, the cottage looked deserted save for the lingering smell of tea that wafted through the air.

A feeble voice from the backroom beckoned, "Welcome, my dear Morgana. I suppose you have come to demand answers of a dying woman."

"No," replied Morgana as she followed the voice to where Eloise lay. She was but a corpse on the massive bed. Her vacant eyes peered over the covers.

"I have come to offer forgiveness," Morgana continued.

Her words were met with hoarse laughter. Eloise did not seek forgiveness, let alone believe she was in need of it. So deeply was she entrenched in the darkness, she had long since lost touch with her conscience. Her only desire was for Morgana to ask about the quest. Ever since that fateful day when Morgana broke the dream lover's spell, Eloise had lain in bed, growing weaker and weaker, waiting for Morgana. Her powers all but gone, she clung to her hold on Morgana as the last remnant of her glory. She had power, at least, over Morgana through her knowledge of all that had transpired.

"Are you not curious what happened that day?" Eloise goaded.

"I know what I need to," Morgana replied. "Do *you*?"

Vexed at the challenge, Eloise pushed herself up in bed and began hotly, "*You* know nothing. You never have. That is your problem. You are too weak to ask the right questions and too blind to see the answers, even when they are right in front of your face."

"I could say the same for you," Morgana cut back. "The answers have been right in front of both of us all along. *I* see them now. May *you* see them before you die."

With that, Morgana flipped her hand and a large mirror appeared before Eloise, shutting out view of all else.

"What foolishness is this?" Eloise questioned as she saw herself in the mirror, old, ugly, and evil.

Then the mirror flashed, and she saw instead an image of Lilian lying lifeless in a boat. Her beautiful hair was matted about her pale face. The boat floated through the mist until it came to rest at the water's edge. The Lady Nimue glided over and held Lilian by the hand. Blood instantly flowed through her frozen body, and her face began to glow with a luminous light. Lilian smiled, opened her eyes, and sat up.

"Where am I?" she asked dreamily.

"You are in the Vale of Avalon," Nimue replied. "The place where souls are purified with grace upon grace and given new life."

"Why have I come hither?" Lilian asked in a puzzled voice.

"You have been chosen to be a Grail Maiden of the Lord," Nimue explained. "Will you accept this calling? Mind you, it is wrought with danger and hardship."

"If it pleases the Lord," Lilian replied. "I accept whatever calling He giveth me."

As the words flowed from her mouth, a great light began to shine forth from Nimue's hands. She appeared to be holding something sacred and presenting it to Lilian.

"Drink," Nimue said.

"The Holy Grail!" Eloise exclaimed, grasping toward the mirror, but the scene disappeared before the goblet came into full view. She was left only with the horrid image of her own reflection. She wailed, "I was so close! Bring it back! Bring it back!"

Morgana said a prayer of blessing amidst Eloise's harsh cries and then departed—in peace.

AUTHOR'S BIOGRAPHY

Stephanie McGann is a writer and teacher in the classical tradition. Her work is inspired by her faith, her family, and her students. Follow her blog at www.classicalteachersjournal.com.

www.ingramcontent.com/pod-product-compliance
Lightning Source LLC
Chambersburg PA
CBHW021045130626
46552CB00005B/2015